INTERCEPTING SYDNEY

MCKINNEY ENTERPRISES SEATTLE
BOOK 1

JESI HAYNES

RESILIENT
Embers
PUBLISHING

Editor: Pauline Harris

Paperback ISBN: 978-1-970345-00-1

Digital ISBN: 978-1-970345-01-8

Published by Resilient Embers Publishing.

Visit the author's website: www.jesihaynes.com

*For my mom, who gave me a love of reading very early
And for my bonus mom, who modeled healthy
relationships and kept romance books on the shelves.
This book wouldn't exist without both of them.*

"You're late," Chantelle hissed as Sydney walked into the brightly lit kitchen. Sydney flinched and opened the fridge, pulling out a carton of eggs and butter. With the ease of years of practice, Sydney slid a pan onto the stove, turned on the burner, and pulled out a loaf of fresh bread.

Chantelle twirled around on her stool like a child, as if she hadn't just celebrated her twenty-first birthday. Her long, blonde hair swirled around her as she spun. Sydney cracked the eggs into the pan and dropped bread into the toaster. Chantelle picked up a pale pink envelope from the counter. She held it up to the light to try to see through it and then hid it again under her fashion magazine.

Sydney's heart caught. It had been months since her younger sister Ava's last letter, and Sydney anxiously awaited each one. She wanted that letter more than anything. Ava's letters were filled with the mundane, the routine of her life at boarding school, but they meant much more. A letter meant Ava was doing well.

She flipped the eggs with finesse as her stepmom entered the room and sat beside Chantelle at the counter. Not a hair was out of place, and she wore a classic black suit and teal blouse. Gold bracelets on her wrist tinkled against each other.

The beaming smile Belinda had for her daughter morphed into a deep frown as she addressed Sydney. "I do hope this tardiness won't become a habit. We cannot be late for work. You're aware of your responsibilities and the consequences for shirking them."

"Yes, ma'am," Sydney replied. She was very well aware and remembered every threat Belinda had ever made. They ranged from simply withholding Ava's letters, to cutting the power to her room, to threatening to release Ava to foster care. For years now, Sydney toiled and did anything and everything asked of her in order to keep Ava safely tucked away at school.

She plated the perfectly cooked over easy eggs with crisp buttered toast and served Belinda first. Within minutes, Chantelle's breakfast was ready as well. Sydney poured orange juice for Chantelle and coffee for Belinda, just as they liked it, and poured an additional coffee for Belinda's latest husband, Tad. Moments later, he walked into the kitchen, grabbed his mug, and returned to his home office without a word to anyone.

After they finished their meals, Belinda grabbed her purse from the counter and stalked through the house and out to the garage. The door slammed behind her.

When they were alone, Sydney took the opportunity to ask, "May I have my letter, please?"

Chantelle laughed. "I have no idea what you're talking about." She flounced from the room with her magazine and the letter in hand.

Sydney wanted to go after her, but any commotion would garner Tad's attention, and that would be worse. On a whim, he could decide to fire her from his restaurants, and that would put Sydney out on the streets and Ava into foster care. Her biggest fear, the thing that kept her going every day, was letting Ava down. She hadn't seen her sister in years, but she was the only real family Sydney had left. Ava was the most important person in her life, and she would do everything in her power to make sure she had stability and a good education.

Sydney gritted her teeth and washed the breakfast dishes. Half of Belinda's meal was still on her plate. Sydney had tried once to make her a smaller meal, and she lost the privilege of her bus pass for a week for her thoughtlessness.

Living with Belinda, Tad, and Chantelle wasn't so bad most of the time. Sydney made their breakfasts and was responsible for cleaning, but then she went to work and didn't have to think about them. She had her own room, which she collapsed into at the end of each exhausting day. Ava would be graduating soon and turning eighteen later in the year. Sydney just had to hang on a little longer, and then they could leave Tad and Belinda behind and figure out their futures together.

With the dishes clean, dried, and put away, Sydney

grabbed her own lunch and rushed out the door to catch her bus to one of Tad's restaurants. He owned three restaurants in the city, as well as a large event space that was gaining in popularity. The space was beautiful and popular for weddings, charity events, and other community gatherings. Sydney spent most days hidden away washing dishes, cleaning floors, and removing grease from kitchen surfaces at one or more of the four businesses.

The restaurant she was assigned to for the day was the trendiest place in the city. It opened a year earlier to great acclaim. It was called, simply, Black. The name was a mystery to everyone, because it had nothing to do with the concept of the restaurant. There wasn't a single black surface in the establishment. It also wasn't ironically white. The place was furnished in shades of blue, from the robin's egg blue floor to the navy wall treatments and midnight tablecloths. The dishes that she would spend all evening washing were a striking canary yellow.

At this time of day, though, she helped out with setting the restaurant up for opening, making sure everything was in order for service. Everything had to be perfect here, and she appreciated the concentration it took to complete her assigned tasks. Once the dishwashing started in earnest, her mind had time to wander, and she desperately wanted to know what Ava had written in her letter.

Ava was nearly ten years younger than Sydney. Their mom had died weeks after Ava was born, and Sydney tried to be the best big sister she could. She adored Ava from the moment she was born. A few years later, their father met Belinda and Chantelle. They were a happy family for a few years until Sydney and Ava tragically lost their father to a heart attack. It didn't take Belinda long to remarry, and they'd been at Tad's mercy ever since.

Ava was sent to boarding school within a month of Belinda's remarriage, and she had written Sydney a letter nearly every month until recently. Sydney was becoming increasingly anxious about what would happen when Ava graduated. Belinda hadn't said a word about it, and Sydney wondered if she even remembered how old Ava was. She was only a few years younger than Chantelle, but she had been placed out of sight and out of mind. Ava's name was only ever mentioned to keep Sydney in line.

Sydney hung on every word she received from Ava, reading every letter over and over. There wasn't much about friends in her letters, but she often shared what she was learning, what she thought of her teachers, and what projects she was working on. Ava was a good student and enjoyed school, which Sydney clung to whenever she was having a difficult day. As long as Ava was happy, she could keep moving forward.

Sydney picked up a rack of martini glasses and turned to take them to the bar when another employee came around a corner too quickly and slammed into her. She tried to right herself, but she watched the rack slip and topple as if in slow motion. Every glass in the rack hit the floor in a loud crash of shattered glass. Her co-worker paled, backed away, and rushed from the room, leaving her to deal with the cleanup.

Tad burst into the kitchen, took one look at the mess, and yelled at her to clean it up before someone got hurt. She jerked into motion and gathered what she needed to clean up the thousands of tiny pieces of glass. Tears sprang to her eyes as she mentally estimated the cost of the broken glasses. Tad would surely schedule her to work extra hours to make up for it. There would be no arguing that it wasn't her fault.

Tad disappeared back into the front of house to return to greeting guests. Not one other employee in the kitchen even looked over, much less offered to help or commiserate. This wasn't the first time and wouldn't be the last. She wished it had happened at the diner instead of Black, though. These custom martini glasses with yellow woven through the stems and dark blue rims were much more expensive than the simple glasses used at the diner.

Sydney swiped at the tears and made quick work of cleaning up the mess. When each shard of glass was swept up and thrown away, she looked up to find the dishwashing area stacked high with the tiny yellow plates that every appetizer was served on, more martini glasses, and dozens of wine glasses. Before she could even start on those, she had to trek down to the basement for a new case of the glasses that had broken.

She hated the basement in this building. The stairs

were a hazard, and the only reason the city allowed the restaurant to remain open was money and Tad's assurance that the basement was never in use. Indeed, the door remained locked at all times, but Sydney had a key. She was the designated person to navigate through the maze of the back room, unlock the nearly hidden door, and brave the rickety stairs into the dimly lit basement.

The large area was used for storage of wine and glassware, as well as old linens, furniture, and decades of dust. Deliveries were made using an exterior door at the building next door, and there was a tunnel between the two buildings. Ingenious really, but as a practical matter, Sydney hated it. At the bottom of the stairs, she took a deep breath and regretted it as she was overcome with a coughing fit. Once she could breathe again, she picked her way across the room and found a case of the right glasses and hefted it back up the stairs.

She took care to lock the door and sorted the new glasses into the dishwasher to deliver to the bartenders as quickly as possible. She worked her way through the rest of the dishes, finishing well after closing. She was one of the last people in the building by the time she stepped out into the freezing darkness and trudged her way back to the bus stop.

When she got home, the house was dark, as usual. She slipped up the stairs without making a sound and got ready for bed. Her body ached with exhaustion, and she wanted nothing more than to sleep, but her mind wouldn't rest. Her room in the attic was so cold that her breath turned to visible vapor in the air, but she had accumulated a nice nest of blankets, warm socks, and sweats.

She didn't want Ava to come home and live like this with her. Ava needed somewhere to go when she graduated. Somewhere safe and healthy. Somewhere she could make her own choices and do great things.

TWO

WARD

Ward stepped out of the executive elevator on the twenty-third floor of the McKinney Building and into the large, open space shared by his assistant to the left and his father's assistant to the right.

"Good morning, Marian," he greeted his silver-haired assistant.

"Good morning, Mr. McKinney."

Ward pushed through his office door behind her. She'd been his assistant for over a year, and she greeted him the same way every day. In his mind, Mr. McKinney was his father, but she'd refused to call him Ward, and he'd stopped asking.

As he sat and brought his computer to life, Marian entered with a cup of coffee for him and her notepad. She sat in the chair facing his desk, and Ward raised an eyebrow. There was rarely enough to discuss to warrant sitting.

"Thank you for the coffee. What's on the agenda today?" He found their routine comforting, even though he checked his calendar in the elevator every morning and knew exactly what to expect for the day.

She tapped her pen against her notepad, her eyes wandering around the room.

"Marian? What's wrong?"

Her gaze shot up to meet his, and her professional mask slipped back into place. "You have the Tate lunch at 1 p.m. this afternoon. I sent you everything I could find. If you don't mind my nosiness, he seems a little desperate. It isn't a good look."

Ward nodded. He'd only skimmed the pages of documentation so far, but he would dig into it deeper this morning. So far, it looked like this lunch would be a waste of time.

"I also RSVPed you for the New Hope gala next week with a plus one. I trust you'll have one."

He nodded again. Charity galas were insufferably boring solo. They were only marginally better with a beautiful woman on his arm. Marian ran through a few other mundane items on her list and stood to leave.

"Wait," Ward said, stopping her in her tracks. "There's something bothering you." She'd been fidgety and hadn't met his eyes throughout most of their meeting. His gut filled with unease, which only got worse when she finally looked at him and revealed the shine of tears in her eyes.

She took a shaky breath. "My sister had a fall last night. She's at the hospital in Chicago, and they're planning surgery on her hip in the morning. I'm sorry, Mr. McKinney, but—"

"You're going. Take the jet. Bring her back here. Seattle has superior medical care." He was caught off guard by her watery chuckle.

"Thank you. Really. I have a flight booked for tonight, and her doctors are perfectly capable. I have a call in to HR, and they're going to send up a new assistant for you this afternoon so I can spend a little time with her before I go."

Ward tensed and forced himself to take a deep breath before responding. She watched him carefully. "I need you, Marian. You know my track record with assistants. Bring your sister to Seattle."

She backed away and waved a hand at him. "You'll be fine. You're going to pretend this next assistant is me. I'm going on leave, not quitting, but if you're going to be pushy, I'll quit. There are jobs in Chicago." With that, she returned to her desk, closing his office door behind her.

Ward dropped back into his chair and grabbed his phone. He texted his best friend and personal bodyguard, Ice.

Did you know about this?

You'll have to be more specific.

Marian is leaving.

> That. Yes. She's going on leave. She'll
> be back. Don't be dramatic. See you at
> 12:30.

Ward dropped his phone back on his desk. He wasn't being dramatic. Marian was the first assistant that had lasted longer than two weeks. Some hadn't even lasted an hour. She was the first one that he respected and trusted. She did her job and did it well. She didn't take any nonsense from him, and she made his job easier.

Plenty of people believed he was nothing more than the son of the CEO. That he hadn't earned his place here at his father's side. That he didn't work hard every day to continue to grow their enterprise and prove them wrong. Fueled by determination, Ward shoved thoughts of his assistant aside. He skimmed his email and returned his attention to the Tate file.

A few hours later, his door opened and Ice let himself in. As usual, he was dressed the same as Ward in a classic, tailored, black suit, ready to fit in at Ward's side wherever the day took them. Ward stood and stretched. He grabbed his tablet and phone and followed Ice back out of his office. He paused when he noticed the new young woman at Marian's side.

"Good timing, Mr. McKinney. This is Lacey. She'll take care of everything while I'm gone."

Ward nodded and continued on to the elevator. He'd barely glanced at Lacey, but he didn't need to. He could feel her eyes burning a hole through him and breathed a sigh of relief when the elevator doors closed.

"That was ruder of you than usual," Ice commented.

"She won't last. Why bother?"

Ice shook his head. "She won't last if you're rude to her. Self-fulfilling prophecy."

"I have an idea. You're always here. You can be my assistant while Marian is gone."

"Not a chance," Ice replied without a hint of a smile.

Ward shrugged. It was the answer he'd expected. He trusted Ice with his life, and his security position suited him. They'd met in college and both graduated with the same business degree. Ward tried to take advantage of Ice's intelligence whenever he was receptive, but he was never going to be happy in a desk job.

As they settled into Ice's sleek, silver BMW, Ward's phone buzzed with a text from Marian.

> Be nice to Lacey. And don't call me while I'm gone. She can handle whatever I would have done for you.

"Does she even know me? I'm not nice to anyone," Ward muttered.

"Maybe you should think about changing that."

"Next thing I know, you'll be suggesting I join a monastery."

Ice laughed. "Right. That'd make my job obsolete, and I'd lose my best friend to a vow of silence, so no. But I am feeling too old to keep chasing you around nightclubs. Are you on a mission to have a photo with a different girl in the tabloids every day for a year or something?"

Ward wasn't up for arguing with Ice about this again.

He didn't mind the photographers or the women that liked to hang on him—in fact, he encouraged them. No matter how many times they'd been over it, the argument never changed. Ice wanted him to stop opening himself up to being used by random women. Ward wasn't interested in an actual relationship. Indulging in the company of a beautiful woman that knew she wouldn't get anything more from him than a drink and a photo op seemed like a harmless way to keep the paparazzi busy. The tabloid photos kept him in the spotlight, reminding everyone in the business community of his success. Win, win.

They pulled up in front of the restaurant, and Ice handed the keys to the valet. Once inside, Ice took a seat at the bar while Ward found Robert Tate at a table along the back wall. The other man stood and wiped his hand on his khaki pants before shaking Ward's hand. Ward barely hid his cringe.

As they took their seats, Ward studied Robert. He seemed to be aging more rapidly than Ward. Robert had gained a receding hairline and a growing waistline over the last ten years.

"It's good to see you. It's been a long time," Robert said.

"It has. College feels like a lifetime ago. I understand you're looking for an investor, and you think I should invest." Nostalgia wasn't going to get Robert very far. Ward remembered him, of course. They'd been in many of the same business classes and ran into each other frequently. Robert had also been heir to a family business. Based on the information Marian compiled, he was running it into the ground.

Robert blinked, taken aback at the abrupt shift to business. The waiter appeared before he could respond.

"What can I get you gentlemen to drink?"

"IPA?" Robert asked. The waiter nodded.

"Scotch. Neat."

The waiter rattled off the specials and left them to consider the menus. Ward left his unopened on the table. He'd already made his decision. Nothing he'd seen so far gave him confidence that Robert had any kind of ace up his sleeve. He raised an eyebrow when Robert ogled a waitress serving a table across the room.

A wedding band glinted on Robert's finger. "How's your wife?" Ward asked.

Robert's eyes jolted back to Ward. "She's a frazzled mom of three. It doesn't hurt to look. I know you understand. I've seen the tabloids."

Ward tilted his head as if considering the comment. "The difference is that I was smart enough to avoid marriage. Are you going to get to the point of this meeting, or should I go?" He shifted as if to leave, and Robert raised a hand to stop him.

The waiter brought their drinks and quickly left. "Yes, yes, of course." Robert took a long sip of his beer. I have a lead on a big project. I don't have the capital to do it alone and thought you might be interested."

"I'm always interested in making money. I'm listening." He settled into his chair.

Robert enthusiastically shared his vision for a real

estate development on the south side of town. He gestured widely as he painted a picture of a gleaming multi-use building and the glamorous people that would call it home. It was an area of the city Ward was well acquainted with, and for the right investor it could indeed be a profitable opportunity.

Ward interrupted him, "I get it. The project is appealing. Why should I do it with you?"

Robert took another sip of beer. "Our firm has decades of experience successfully running projects like this. This should be an easy decision for you."

"Oh, it is." Ward opened his tablet to a report that showed Robert's company's string of losses over the last few years. He turned it so that Robert could see the screen. "This your company?"

Robert paled and sat back. "There have been extenuating circumstances. I'm not asking you to invest in the firm, just in the project. A thirty percent return on investment is virtually guaranteed."

Ward shook his head and tossed back the rest of his scotch. "I don't think so. Thanks for the drink. Good to see you." He pushed back and walked out of the restaurant with Ice on his heels, leaving Robert sputtering.

Once back in the car, Ice asked, "Did you take the meeting just to see him sweat, or did you actually consider the proposal?"

Ward shrugged. "I wanted to hear more about what he was planning. It's a good project. I want it. But not with him."

Once back at the office, they parted ways at the lobby.

Ward tensed when he found Lacey alone at his assistant's desk. He ignored her and closed himself in his office. The rest of the day, he handled the things that demanded his attention, but his mind was on that piece of property. The area could benefit from some new development, and a multi-use building was almost guaranteed to be lucrative.

At precisely 5:00, there was a light tap on his door. Lacey opened it without waiting for his response.

"I wanted to check to see if you'll need anything else this evening?" she asked, with a little too much emphasis on *anything*.

"No."

She waited a beat for him to say something else. When he didn't, she backed up and replied, "Okay, well, I'll see you in the morning."

As the door closed, he muttered, "Not if I can help it." The door had barely latched when it opened again and Ice walked in, his suit jacket slung over his shoulder.

"No," Ice said.

"What?"

"Do not fire the new assistant. I'm sure she's fine. Let's go hit the gym."

Ward leaned his head back and closed his eyes. "Fine," he huffed and stood, gathering his things to leave. "But if she hints any harder at being open to after hours activities tomorrow, you owe me twenty bucks and a day as my assistant."

Ice scowled at him. "Your cynicism shouldn't surprise me anymore, yet it does."

"It's a curse, and I've made peace with it, you know that. Women have absolutely no interest in knowing anything about me yet want to be seen with me. I know the score, and I can live with it. My dad made the mistake of thinking one was different, and he paid for it."

"He got *you* out of that relationship, and he's in a long-term relationship again. I think he came out okay."

THREE

SYDNEY

Sydney waited three long days for Chantelle to hand over Ava's letter. Three days of wondering how her sister was doing and knowing the answers were just out of reach. Three days of trying to figure out how to convince Chantelle to release the pink envelope.

When Sydney got home from a long day of work at the diner, Chantelle was dancing around the living room with a huge smile on her face. Sydney saw her opportunity and rushed to the kitchen, all traces of exhaustion gone. She mixed up a quick batch of fudge brownies and slipped them into the oven.

"Good day?" she asked when Chantelle danced into the kitchen.

"The best!" Chantelle gushed. "Mom said there will be an office assistant job for me soon, and I can't wait! You should see who I'll be working for." She twirled and eyed Sydney. "You wouldn't appreciate him, but he's so hot. Like, seriously, he could be a model." She fanned herself, and Sydney ignored the dig. She was right. Sydney didn't have time to appreciate men or the freedom to consider a relationship.

Chantelle beamed. "Mom said he's grumpy with his assistants, but I know I can win him over. I'm awesome." Belinda worked in Human Resources at some big company, and she must have decided it was time for Chantelle to earn her own money. Sydney didn't care, but she kept Chantelle talking until the brownies were ready.

When she pulled them out of the oven and the sweet smell wafted through the kitchen, Chantelle's mouth dropped open. "Hey, Chantelle, I won't tell Belinda that you have this pan of deliciousness if you give me the pink envelope that you've been hiding." Chantelle nodded slowly and looked around as if checking for Belinda. She rushed to her room and she was back in moments with the envelope. She tossed it on the counter, carefully wrapped the brownie pan in a towel, and carried it away.

Sydney didn't hesitate to grab the envelope and rush upstairs. The extra effort to make the dessert and listen to Chantelle prattle on was worth it. Back in her room, she curled up in bed with Ava's letter, took a deep breath, and opened it.

> Syd,
> Have you forgotten me? I'm stressing out here. I haven't gotten a letter from you since

September. I guess you're busy with your own life.
I get it, but I don't know what to do, and I
need you.

I've been applying to colleges. I've been
working so hard to have the grades to qualify for
some scholarships, but my guidance counselor
said I'm not good enough. What am I going to do
if I don't go to school? Where am I going to live?
Everyone here has big plans for Ivy League
schools. Students aren't allowed to have jobs
here, so I don't have any experience to support
myself.

Please write. Tell me it'll be okay. Or tell me to
run away and join the circus, if that's my fate. I
don't have any special talents, so I'll be cleaning
up after the elephants if you come looking for me.

Love you. Miss you.
Ava

Sydney couldn't control the tears that streamed down her face. She didn't understand how it could be possible that Ava hadn't received a letter from her in several months. Sydney replied to every letter. She wrote Ava every month, as Belinda allowed. But Belinda was in control of mailing them, and she must be withholding them. Was she reading their letters?

It had always bothered Sydney that she wasn't allowed to seal and mail them herself. Belinda had never shared the name or address of the school with Sydney, and Ava had never included that information in her letters. The pink envelopes that she received Ava's letters in were always blank and unsealed.

She didn't receive a letter every month, and she thought the same, that Ava was just busy. But maybe Ava shared something she wasn't supposed to, and Belinda confiscated her letters too. The more she thought about it, the surer she was that Belinda was up to something. She hadn't written anything in the last several months that should cause her letters to be withheld, unless Belinda was withholding them out of spite and viciousness.

She re-read Ava's letter a dozen times. She wished she had the answers. She didn't know what Ava would do next either. She certainly didn't want her to come home, to work for Tad, and walk on eggshells as Sydney did. Even if she did have a suggestion, she was sure her letter wouldn't make it to her sister. She had to find out, somehow, where she was and get a message to her. A real, uncensored message. It seemed hopeless.

She couldn't lose hope, though. She hadn't worked as hard as she had to give up now. She was determined for Ava to have a better life. She could do this. She could find a way to save her sister. Searching the house might turn up something that would give her a clue where her sister was. There was a big problem with that, though. She was never home alone. She worked all day and late into the evening, and when she was home, so was everyone else. There was no time for snooping. The few times she had been truly sick, Chantelle had been tasked with watching over her. At the time, she'd thought that was a small act of kindness. Now, she saw it for the supervision it was, and her sorrow turned to anger.

Ava could be anywhere. She may not even be in the same state. Sydney pulled out all of her old letters once more. She poured over them looking for clues. Nothing jumped out at her now any more than before. In the winter, Ava occasionally mentioned snow, but there was snow here too. It ruled out some southern states but didn't help much. Christmas was celebrated at her school as a Christian holiday, so it could be a religious school, but it didn't necessarily have to be.

Sydney carefully put the letters away in the secret panel under a floorboard. She flopped back into bed. She wouldn't lose hope. She would have faith that answers would present themselves and that she would find words to reassure her sister without having yet another letter go missing. But for now, she'd give in to the sorrow for just a little while as she fell into a fitful sleep.

FOUR

WARD

Ward couldn't take it anymore. He'd put up with Lacey for several days, and he thought Marian might be proud of him, but he couldn't take her advice any longer. She'd said to treat Lacey the same way he'd treat her. That was impossible. Lacey wouldn't stay out of his office. He'd tried to set boundaries. He explained that he and Marian only met briefly in the morning and she left him alone the rest of the day. Lacey had smiled and nodded at him and promptly reappeared an hour later with a fresh coffee or a pastry. He had a dozen pastries hardening in the trash under his desk right now. She hadn't hinted again at joining him after hours, so he hadn't even won his bet with Ice. With the constant interruptions, he hadn't gotten any work done and was at his wit's end.

Ward looked up at the ceiling and took a deep breath. He picked up the phone and made a call.

"HR, how can I help you, Mr. McKinney?"

"Lacey needs to go. I'm sure she would be a great assistant for someone, but she needs to be reassigned."

"Yes, sir. I'll have her replaced first thing in the morning."

That accomplished, Ward turned his attention back to the projects he had in progress. Most were coming along well, but there were a couple that needed his focus. When Lacey popped her head in one more time, Ward lost it. He grabbed his stuff, brushed past her, and headed for the elevator. He called Ice on the way down.

Ward didn't give Ice the chance to say anything before blurting, "I'm going to work from home. No need to follow me."

"I'll give you an hour. You'll be itching to go out. What's wrong with your office?"

Ward's phone buzzed, and he pulled it away from his ear. His father's name appeared on the screen. "I'll call you back."

He answered the other call and held his breath.

"In my office, Ward."

Ward closed his eyes. He'd been so close to escaping. "I'll be right there," he promised as he hit the button to send the elevator back up. When he stepped out of the elevator, Lacey was packing up her things in tears, and his father's assistant was scowling at him. She waved him into his father's office. He paused and took a deep breath before opening the door.

"You wanted to see me?" Ward asked as he crossed the room and dropped into a chair, knowing full well what this was about.

Russell sat back in his chair, his fingers steepled against his chin. "I thought you'd broken your short-term assistant streak."

"Marian is on leave, so I seem to be back in the young, thoughtless assistant revolving door. HR should know better."

"Ward, you have to stop. Grow up and deal with it. You're over thirty. You're an executive. I know some of these girls lack maturity, but everyone starts learning somewhere. They aren't born Marians—they're trained, and it takes more than three days."

"They should be learning before they get to me. This one was in my office literally every hour. I tried patience. I tried clearly setting times to meet. I can't work like this." At the expression on his father's face, Ward was becoming increasingly aware that he sounded immature himself. Shame churned in his gut.

"Whoever they send you tomorrow is it. Deal with whatever quirks they have until you get your assistant back, and when she does come back, make sure she knows how much you appreciate her."

Ward nodded and sighed. "Topic change?"

"Sure." Russell leaned forward, a spark of interest in his eyes, replacing the disappointment that had been there.

Ward filled him in on his meeting earlier in the week with Robert Tate. "The more that I look into it, the more I want that project. He's got a few other interesting projects going on, but a bunch of garbage in his portfolio as well."

"And how worrisome is the garbage?"

"Enough that I don't think there's a reason to partner with him. I'd rather do it on our own, but I'm working on that analysis now. Or I was trying to, in between interruptions."

Russell nodded. "I'm intrigued. I trust your judgement, Ward. At least when it comes to making money."

Ward's chest lightened a little at the compliment. "Thanks, Dad." He stood. "If we're done here, I'm going to head home and see what I can dig up."

Russell stood and stretched. "Remember what I said about your next assistant. The revolving door isn't a good look for a leader in this company. The tabloids aren't either."

Ward wanted to argue that last point. His reputation kept reminding people that their company was there, successful, important. He wore his eligible bachelor status like a badge of pride. His father may be older now, and settled, but Ward was determined to enjoy this phase of his life.

ICE WAS RIGHT. After spending a couple of hours focused on data and spreadsheets, Ward was ready to get out into the noise and motion of the club scene. As if Ice had read his mind, he walked into Ward's kitchen, twirling his keys around his finger. "Ready?" he asked.

Ward grinned. "Let's do it."

In the car, Ice asked, "What'll it be tonight? The new

EDM club down near the water, or the 80s nostalgia bar?"

Ward looked at him incredulously. "80s? Really? Who are you, and what have you done with my friend?"

Ice chuckled and shrugged. "Just trying to shake up your life a little."

Ward shook his head. "The day I agree to a nostalgia anything is the day you can put me in the ground."

In minutes, they were in front of one of his favorite clubs. Inside, the music was loud enough that the beat resonated in his chest. It drowned out the constant noise in his head. He wasn't here to drink. He was here to get lost in the music, to feel the buzz, the vibration of the bass under his skin. The beautiful women were a perk, and it wasn't long before there were a few sticking close to him, lost in the beat themselves.

After a few songs, he disentangled himself and found Ice at the bar. "Thanks for putting up with this. I know you hate it," Ward admitted.

Ice glanced at him and handed him a water. "It's my job. And you're my friend. But I won't complain when you're ready to leave."

Ward nodded, downed the water, and returned to the dance floor for another few songs before putting Ice out of his misery and leaving with a woman on his arm. He did nothing more than walk her to her car, but the paparazzi didn't care. The photos of them leaving together were all the "journalists" were interested in.

FIVE

SYDNEY

Sydney was no closer to any solutions. She was working another mind-numbing shift at Black, carefully handling the fragile stemware to avoid the repercussions of breaking any more. The day had started with a shift at the diner, where she got a call from Tad demanding to know why she wasn't at Black for opening. She had never shown up to the wrong location without it being due to Tad jerking her around. It was happening more and more frequently, and she genuinely didn't know if Tad was losing control or if he was deliberately sabotaging her.

She should be used to standing for long, strenuous hours, but her feet and back ached. She had barely eaten all day. The biggest festival of the year was going on throughout the city, and every bar and restaurant would be packed all weekend, including the diner and Black.

While her hands kept busy moving dishes in and out of the dishwasher, Sydney thought back to the festivals before her father died. She always loved going down to the waterfront with her dad and Ava to watch the fireworks. They were loud, but the explosions of color were so beautiful against the dark night sky. They would stop for a slice of pizza and cotton candy and walk past the booths where artisans sold their jewelry and trinkets. Her father was always patient when she wanted to stop and look at the varied creations for sale, marveling at the creativity on display. Now, Sydney couldn't remember the last time she was able to stop and enjoy something for the beauty of it.

She sighed, completed her tasks, and hung her apron on a hook in the locker room. As she left the employee area, she walked down the dimly lit hall past Tad's office, toward the front of the restaurant. A few people lingered outside the restrooms farther down, and a man in a suit stumbled toward her. She moved to the side to allow him to pass, but he veered much too close.

Before she realized what was happening, he grabbed her arms and pinned her against the wall. His hot, intoxicated breath huffed in her face, and his hands moved down her arms to her waist. He squeezed hard enough to cause pain, and he pressed his body against hers. She shuddered in revulsion, and her heart raced.

"I'll admit, you're not quite what I asked for, but you'll do," he muttered against her cheek, his words slurred. One of his hands moved up to her chest, grabbing her breast painfully.

Sydney tried to jerk away, but there was nowhere to go. She had the wall at her back, and his grip was too strong to move him to the side. Despite her fear, she tried to stay calm. "You have me confused for someone else. Please let me go," she asked with a confidence she didn't feel. She blinked back tears from the pain of his bruising grip.

"I don't think so. I was promised some entertainment." One of his hands wandered lower as his teeth nipped at her earlobe. Sydney pushed on his chest, and when that was unsuccessful, she pulled her knee up as hard as she could. She shoved away as soon as she made contact. He stumbled back in pain, cursing loudly. She rushed back the way she had come and ran straight into Tad. She looked up at him with relief, but it was short lived at the furious expression on his face.

"What have you done?" he roared at her, grabbing her by the wrist and slamming her into the wall. Her head hit the surface so hard she saw stars, and she choked back sobs. "How dare you assault a VIP?" Tad kept a punishing grip of her wrist and pulled her along as he rushed over to check on the man, paying no mind to her stumbling over her own feet in his wake. "I apologize for this one's behavior. I'll make it right."

His grip tightened even more, and she feared he was about to break her wrist. He started waving his other arm and shouting instructions for other employees to accommodate whatever this person wanted. When the commotion started to settle and he dragged her back to his office, Sydney found herself truly afraid of what might happen next. Two large men lurked just inside his office, and fear took over. She surprised Tad with a sharp stomp to his instep, and she ran like hell when his grip on her wrist loosened.

She rushed out through the back exit and into the icy night air. Sydney ran down the dark alleyway between buildings. The door slammed against the wall as someone burst out behind her. Her lungs burned. She ran out into the street, which was filled with people enjoying the festival. She had never been so glad for the streets to be full. She pushed through the crowd, trying to get as much distance between herself and whoever was chasing her as possible.

While she didn't think Tad himself was chasing her, the other two men in his office looked muscular and capable of dragging her back. She rushed as much as she could through the crowd toward the open park where everyone was gathering for the evening's fireworks. Just as she turned to try to see if she was still being followed, someone grabbed her and pulled her around the side of a building, a warm hand over her mouth. Fear that hadn't abated still coursed through her, and Sydney couldn't make sense of the words she was hearing close to her ear. She struggled, but the deep voice was calm and insistent.

What registered first was that he wasn't trying to take her anywhere. He was blocking her in against the wall and had a light hand over her mouth, but he wasn't pressing himself against her. He wasn't doing anything but talking to her, and his voice was steady and patient. She finally started to hear his words.

"It's okay. You're safe. I don't know you. I don't know who you're running from. I just want to help." He repeated the words over and over as her breathing calmed and she finally met his gray eyes. At her eye contact, he eased his hand away. "The way you're darting between people is causing a ripple in the crowd. If there's someone you're running from, they're going to see the trail plain as day. Let me help you blend in, and they'll go right by."

Stupid. She felt stupid. He was right. She didn't know why he wanted to help her, but she nodded cautiously. "What if they don't go right by?" she asked, a tremor still in her voice.

"Then I'll handle it." She wanted to trust his confidence more than anything.

Someone coughed beside them, and they both looked over toward a man standing with his back to them.

"Okay, Ice will handle it."

Sydney frowned. "Ice?"

"Private security," he replied. He took his jacket off and then the gray hoodie beneath it. He dropped the hoodie over her head and shrugged his jacket back on, zipping it against the chill. Sydney didn't realize how cold she had been until she was enveloped in the warmth of his sweater. He pulled the hood up over her head and carefully tucked her blonde hair into it to further hide her identity.

Sydney studied him, but it was too dark to see him clearly. "I'm supposed to know who you are, aren't I?"

He shrugged. "I'm trying to blend in too, and I'm not doing a very good job if you do."

He took the ball cap that Ice handed over with a roll

of his eyes, and then he led her casually out into the crowd, his hand warm, firm, but gentle around hers.

Fireworks began shooting up into the sky, and Sydney's breath caught in her chest. She didn't know where they were going, but it didn't matter, as they were moving deeper into the crowd. They stopped closer to the water where the view was spectacular. Tears slipped down Sydney's cheeks. The man stood behind her, holding her left hand with his and intertwining their fingers. The warmth of that connection grounded her. With his right hand, he held on lightly to a belt loop at her hip, under the hoodie that was much too big on her. Otherwise, he wasn't touching her, and for the moment, she felt safe.

She tilted her head back to watch the exploding colors in the sky. She winced as her sore head touched his shoulder, but she didn't pull away. Neither did he. He squeezed her hand gently and just stood with her. There was some commotion as people were jostled around them, and she held her breath. As he'd promised, they'd gone right on by. She shuddered and started breathing again.

As the fireworks ended, sadness swept through Sydney. These few minutes with a stranger were the best she'd had in years. It made her feel close to her dad, yet so far from the life she'd had with him. She swiped at her eyes and turned to face the man that had given her a few minutes of peace. People were dispersing around them, and the only one remaining close by was Ice.

"Will you be safe if you go home?" he asked. Sydney

shrugged and remained silent, watching others leave rather than meeting his eyes. She truly didn't know, but that wasn't his problem. Was Tad just intimidating earlier because he'd been drinking and was angry? Would he have hurt her further if she hadn't run? He'd never even touched her before and ignored her most of the time.

"Come on." He led the way out of the park and back toward the businesses lining the street. Ice remained with them on her other side. The men exchanged a look but didn't say anything. They walked a few blocks and entered the lobby of a hotel. Ice left them and approached the desk.

"I can't stay here," Sydney whispered. In the light of the luxurious lobby, she got her first good look of the man she'd held hands with. With the ball cap and casual clothes, it was easy to miss that the man being so kind to her was the infamous Ward McKinney. The man whose face was always featured in the tabloids Chantelle left lying around, the face of a ruthless and sought after businessman. No wonder he had security with him.

He was watching Ice and missed her moment of recognition. "Don't worry," he assured her. "My business keeps a number of rooms here year-round for customers and employees that fly in for meetings. It's a quiet time of year, and we aren't using them all." Ice returned, and they both escorted her up to the eighth floor and down the hall to room 825. Ice made sure the key worked and then handed it to her.

Ward gestured for her to enter. "Feel free to stay as long as you need to, to figure out your next move. Order room service, charge it to the room. Stay safe, okay?" He leaned closer for a moment and dropped his voice. "Thanks for spending time with me. I'm not good at being alone." He smiled and stepped back.

"Thank you," she whispered, addressing both of them. This had been the nicest thing anyone had done for her in a very long time. She was still lost and afraid, but for the moment, she was safe.

Sydney backed into the room and closed the door, peering through the peep hole until Ward and Ice walked away. She rested her forehead against the door for a moment and closed her eyes.

She pulled back and turned to look around the room. It wasn't anything special if you were used to hotel rooms, but for her, it was a warm, comfortable space that she had to herself for the night. There were pretty toiletries in the bathroom and a giant soaking tub with a separate shower. The bed took up the majority of the rest of the room, but there was enough room for a small desk and chair. She peeked through the curtains and watched people still dispersing from the festivities in the street below.

She should go home. She didn't know what awaited her there, but the consequences of not coming home could be bad. She couldn't bring herself to care. This was a treat that she would never expect, and the kindness Ward had shown her was something she wanted to hang on to for just a little while. It was selfish and silly, but her heart wouldn't let go.

A long, hot bath sounded amazing. Her nose and

cheeks were still cold and pink when she looked in the mirror. Ward's sweatshirt helped shield her from the cold, but she was chilled to the bone. The rush of water flowing into the tub soothed Sydney's nerves. She hung Ward's sweater in the small closet and pulled out the white, fluffy robe that waited there. She stepped out of her black pants and shrugged off the black button down shirt she wore to work each day. She eased herself into the steaming tub one inch at a time. She stayed in the tub until the water cooled. Her body relaxed, but her mind did not.

She couldn't shut it off. Every time she tried to turn off a train of thought, it derailed onto another track. She was afraid every time she thought about what had happened at Black. She didn't like the implication that Tad may be selling more than food and alcohol. She was terrified he might have actually intended for her to do whatever that guy had wanted. She wouldn't allow herself to speculate much deeper. She worried about Ava. She needed to find her, to talk to her. She needed to keep her far from Tad.

To distract herself from the fear and uncertainty, her thoughts strayed back to Ward. He had surprised her, both by snatching her off the street and scaring the wits from her, but also by his gentleness and kindness. His confession about not being good at being alone rang true. She'd never seen him alone in a tabloid photo. He always had a beautiful, well-dressed woman on his arm. Sydney was as far as possible from his usual company. She wondered what he had seen in her tonight why he'd made such a drastic move and inserted himself into her life.

She'd never thought much about him when she'd seen his picture in Chantelle's tabloids, but now that she'd met him, she could understand why women clung to him. He was the most attractive man she'd ever interacted with, by far. That wasn't saying much, as she avoided interacting with people as much as possible, but she was still a bit starstruck. It was his confidence, she decided. He did what he wanted, and you couldn't help but go along with it.

Sydney's eye caught on the bruises darkening on her swelling wrist, and she dipped her hand back into the water to hide it from herself for a few minutes longer. She appreciated Ward's gentleness all the more after how roughly Tad had handled her mere minutes earlier.

Sydney ran her fingers over the thin, gold chain she wore around her neck, finding her father's ring and holding it up to the light. It reminded her of better times, of her parents' love. Her dad had a talent for making ordinary things beautiful. She missed him fiercely. She missed the feeling of being safe and loved, of having someone to rely on.

Sydney sighed, and her stomach grumbled. She let the cool water drain from the tub and reluctantly stood and dried herself, wrapping herself in the soft hotel robe. She didn't feel right about taking advantage of room service, but she wasn't about to leave the room to seek out food on her own, and she didn't have any money. She padded out into the room, found the room service information, and called in a simple order for macaroni and cheese and a bottle of water.

Sydney didn't feel comfortable wearing only the robe. She couldn't help but think she might need to leave in a hurry. She dressed in her work clothes once more and couldn't stop herself from putting Ward's hoodie back on. It made her feel like she was wrapped in a hug, even though he'd barely touched her himself.

In minutes, her dinner was delivered, and it looked good, but her stomach was tied in knots. She did her best to eat some of the creamy meal and hydrate. She climbed into bed and fell into an exhausted sleep.

SIX

SYDNEY

The next morning, Sydney woke wrapped in warmth and feeling well rested. She jolted up, suddenly remembering where she was and why. The enormity of running away had panic gripping her lungs. What had she done? What was she going to do now? She had to go back, whatever the consequences. As appealing as it was to disappear and start a new life somewhere now that she'd had a taste of freedom, she couldn't leave without knowing where Ava was. The only person with that knowledge was Belinda.

Sydney stretched and pushed herself out of bed. She flexed her wrist and winced. It was going to hurt for a while, and the discoloration had gotten worse. It didn't seem to be broken, though, and the swelling had gone down. Sydney found her shoes and slipped them on. She looked around the room, partly checking to make sure she wasn't leaving anything behind, but mostly memorizing the room. It had been so nice to get away for a night.

Regardless of what the consequences would be, she couldn't regret it. She set the room key on the desk.

Sydney put her hands in the pocket of Ward's hoodie and froze. She felt something and pulled it out. She was holding more cash than she'd ever held in her life. The bills fanned out, and she counted hundreds of dollars. It probably wasn't much to Ward, but it was a lot to her. She wasn't allowed to have money of her own. Every dollar she earned working for Tad went to Ava's school. Sydney had never once seen a paycheck. She was sure the cash she now held was enough to catch a bus to somewhere else. Eat for a few days. Start over. She swallowed hard and closed her eyes. She was tempted. So tempted.

Instead, she left the room and headed downstairs to the lobby. She asked the clerk at the front desk to direct her to the McKinney building. It was an easy walk of just a few blocks in the bright, cold, morning air.

Once inside the building, she realized she didn't have a plan. She took a deep breath and walked up to the security desk in the bustling lobby. When the overweight, balding man in a uniform looked up, she cleared her throat and said, "I need to see Ward McKinney, please."

He chuckled. "Yeah, that's not going to happen."

"You don't understand. I have something I need to return to him."

He frowned at her. "I can send it up to him, but I can't let you upstairs."

She stood taller and crossed her arms. She wasn't backing down. This was too important. "It's important, and I'm not leaving until I see him."

He stood and leaned over the desk toward her. "I will have you removed. But even if I didn't, you still wouldn't see him. It's not like he walks through the lobby without security."

That gave her an idea. "Security! Yes! Ice knows who I am. Maybe he'll understand. Can I talk to him?"

The security guy's eyebrows would have reached his hairline, if he'd had hair. "No."

She threw her hands up in the air in frustration. He came around the desk and started herding her to the door.

"Seriously, you don't understand. Please don't do this. It's important that I give something back to him. Today. Please."

"What is all the commotion out here?" a quiet but commanding voice demanded, drawing both of their attention. Ice looked more intimidating in his crisp black suit than he had the night before in jeans and a ski jacket, but Sydney was relieved to see him all the same. She would not be deterred.

The security guard sputtered, "Sorry, sir, there's no problem. She was just leaving."

Sydney pushed past him. "No, I wasn't. I need to return something to Ward. It's important."

Ice stared at her for a solid minute, and time seemed to stop. Finally, he nodded and gestured for her to come with him. Sydney breathed a sigh of relief. It was short lived, though, as he took her to a small room off the lobby and closed the door.

He studied her for another minute, his blue eyes narrowed, before asking, "What was so important that you had to make a scene here? Something wrong with the accommodations?"

Sydney jerked back. "No, of course not!" Her voice softened. "I don't have the words to tell you how grateful I am for last night. But, um, I need to return this to Ward." She slipped the hoodie off, making sure the money was still in the pocket.

Ice scowled at her and stepped back, his arms crossed. "He would've asked for it back if it was important."

Sydney hugged it to her chest. "You don't understand."

"Explain it to me. Quickly."

She nodded at his impatience and started talking. "This morning, I found money in the pocket. I need to make sure he gets it all back. Every dollar. I know it probably isn't much to him, but it's a big deal to me." She pleaded with him, "I don't want to hand it off to someone else to return to him and have it get stolen. I don't want him to turn away from the next person that needs his kindness because he thinks they'll just steal from him. It's important."

Ice leaned back against the wall, and he exhaled heavily. He was silent for a long minute. "I can't take you up to him," he raised a hand to stop her from arguing, "but I will personally make sure he gets it. It's the best I can do for you. He's my best friend, and he pays me well. I would never steal from him. You have my word."

Sydney loosened her grip and reluctantly handed it over to Ice. She'd seen the trust between them, and she supposed she should be grateful she'd been able to hand it off to someone Ward trusted. "Thank you," she whispered as she backed toward the door.

"That's it?"

"What do you mean?" she asked, pausing her retreat and glancing back at him.

He shook his head. "You aren't going to ask for anything in return?"

"No?" she replied, confused. "I couldn't possibly ask for anything more. Please thank him again for me, though." She turned to the door but paused. "Actually," she started and turned back toward him.

"Here it comes," he interrupted. "What is it?"

She pulled off the chain that hung around her neck. She rubbed the ring that had been a part of her life since before her father's death and studied it one last time before holding it out to him with shaking hands. "Please ..." She swallowed hard and started again. "Please take this? My father made it when I was little. It's the most precious thing I own."

Ice made no move to take it from her. "Why? You might never see me again."

She willed the tears back and resolutely held her hand out to him, even as it trembled. "I can't keep it safe anymore, and I don't expect to ask for it back. You said Ward pays you well. I have to trust that you wouldn't feel the need to melt it down or carelessly trade it away. That has to be enough. Please."

He finally took the ring from her. He also took the cash from the pocket of the hoodie and handed the sweater back to her. "Keep this. Ward wouldn't want you to freeze out there."

"Thanks," she whispered as she put it back on. He was right, she was shaking, though she wasn't sure it was from the cold. She turned back to the door.

"What's your name?" he asked.

Sydney shook her head and pushed through the door. She walked back through the lobby and ignored the security guard, who smugly called, "Told ya you couldn't go up."

SEVEN

WARD

Ward tried again to read the financial report for a business he was thinking about acquiring. The day of peace he'd hoped for when he arrived to an empty assistant's desk had not materialized. When his phone wasn't ringing, his mind was wandering back to the night before.

The woman had been terrified, and yet she'd put her trust in him. He'd felt ten feet tall. She hadn't known who he was, at least until they reached the hotel. He wanted that feeling back, the feeling of spending time with someone who wasn't there for the money or the photo op. If he admitted it, Ice would say, "I told you so," but spending time with her simply existing and watching fireworks had given him the most peace he'd felt in years.

He was finally fully focused on data analysis when a young blonde in a very short skirt stepped into his office. Her hair lay perfectly straight down her back, and she beamed at him, revealing a bright, perfect smile.

"Good afternoon! I'm Chantelle. I'll be your new assistant. I'm so happy to be working with you!"

Ward remained silent. Her enthusiasm was too much, and he resented the interruption.

"So, um," she shifted her weight from one foot to the other, "what would you like me to do?"

He stared at her for another beat. "Whatever assistants do all day. I'm sure Marian left some sort of notes."

She pouted. "Oh. Okay. I'll just ..." She gestured to the door. He returned his attention to his computer, and she saw herself out, leaving the door wide open. Ward sighed and rubbed his temple.

In less than ten minutes, she was back again, standing in his doorway. He glanced up at her and waited. When he didn't say anything, she asked, "I forgot to ask what I should call you? Mr. McKinney seems awfully formal, but Ward seems too casual."

Ward bristled. He didn't like the way his name sounded on her tongue. She was right. Marian had earned his respect and the right to address him by his first name, even though she refused to use it. But he didn't like being called by his father's name either.

When he took too long to answer, she backed away, her cheerful smile back in place. "That's okay, we'll figure it out. Sir is always appropriate, right?" she asked rhetorically and returned to her desk.

An hour later, his desk phone rang, and he ignored it. It continued ringing. When it stopped, it immediately started again. Ward stood, stretched, and walked to his doorway, observing Chantelle. She had a three-ring binder open on the desk and was reading the contents, using her pencil to follow along word by word across the page. The phone was still ringing.

"Chantelle?" he barked.

She jumped in her chair, and her gaze flew to his. "Yes?"

"Do you hear the phone ringing?"

She tilted her head to the side, listened, and nodded slowly.

When she made no move to act, he prompted, "Shouldn't you answer it?"

"I haven't gotten to that part of the book yet, I'm sorry." She gestured to the binder. It looked like she was on page three or four. At his puzzled expression, she explained, "It's the manual for this job? I haven't gotten to the part that tells me how to answer the phone yet."

The phone stopped ringing, and once again, it started right up again. He growled, "Maybe you should go find that section first." He turned on his heel and went back to his desk. He sighed in relief when she answered the phone.

"Um, hello? Ward McKinney's office?" She paused to listen to the caller. "Yes, he is, one moment."

"No, I'm not," he corrected. "Unless it's my father, I'm not available. Whoever it is can make an appointment."

Her cheeks pinkened. She pressed the hold button to get the caller back. "I'm sorry, you'll need an appointment."

Ward went back to his desk, rubbing his forehead.

His dad was right. He should have stuck it out with Lacey. At least she'd had Marian's guidance for a little while. He pulled up his calendar and groaned. She'd scheduled the caller an appointment for a call in less than hour. He took a deep breath in, counted to four, and let it out slowly. Repeated the calming breath. He forced himself to walk slowly back to her desk. As calmly as possible, he said, "Next time someone wants an appointment, they can wait a week, unless we're working on something urgent for them."

She nodded, hopefully in understanding. "Can I get you some lunch? The book says you like the Chicken Pad Thai from Thai Garden."

"No. Thanks." He closed his office door and sank back into his chair. He perused real estate listings near Tate's new project until it was time to return the call from earlier. He hadn't recognized the name, and the second he placed the call, he realized why. It was a sales person trying to sell him janitorial services for the company. What a waste of his time. He emailed HR and asked them to give Marian a raise. Hopefully her sister's recovery was going well and he could have his competent assistant back soon.

About the time his stomach started rumbling, Chantelle tapped at his door and walked in with a bag from the deli on the corner in her hand. She was frowning at it. "I didn't order it, but lunch arrived for you," she explained as she handed it over.

When he read the notes on the receipt, he smiled. "It's okay, thanks." It was from Ice.

He sent off a text.

> Lunch out of the office would've been better today, but thanks, Ice.

He got back a thumbs-up emoji, and he frowned. Ice was usually more talkative. He'd have to get to the bottom of that later. For now, he had reports to review for an executive meeting later in the week.

Shortly after lunch, Ward's door opened again, but it wasn't Chantelle in the doorway. Ward rose and walked toward the sultry brunette before she could close the door. He held it open as he greeted her. "Lydia, I can't meet right now, but I'm sure my assistant can make you an appointment."

"Oh, no need," she insisted, putting her hand on his arm and kissing the air as he pulled his cheek away. "I just wondered if you needed someone to go with you to the gala this weekend. I have a killer dress I've been dying to wear somewhere special."

"There may still be tickets available, if you'd like to purchase one, but mine is spoken for. Excuse me." He backed away and closed the door in her face. Security in this building was good, but it didn't prevent employees from coming up. He'd never taken a colleague out, and he certainly wasn't going to start with the cougar from marketing.

The rest of the afternoon passed in blissful silence until he heard commotion at his door.

Chantelle insisted, "You have to make an appointment!"

Ice opened the door and slipped past her.

"It's okay, Chantelle. This is Ice. He's security."

"Ready to go?" Ice asked, ignoring the consternation he'd caused.

Ward looked at his watch, startled by the time. "Sure, just a minute." He shut down his computer and grabbed his things. They waved to Chantelle on the way out. She was getting ready to go as well.

Instead of heading to the garage, Ice pressed the lobby button in the elevator. They navigated through the busy lobby and out onto the street. Ward didn't question him. He didn't really care what the plan for dinner was, as long as it was edible. They stepped into a packed Chinese restaurant, and the owner shoved bags of food in their hands before they'd even uttered a word. In moments, they were on their way back to the garage.

"Not eating out tonight?" he asked as they approached the car. Ice shook his head. "What's with you today?"

"Later," Ice muttered. He remained silent until they were sitting at the counter in Ward's kitchen with plates piled high with fried rice and sweet and sour chicken. Ice fiddled with his fork. "Why did you do what you did last night?"

Ward sighed and shrugged. "She was in trouble. I thought I could help."

Ice nodded.

"It was nice to not be me last night. To not be recognized."

Ice nodded again. He reached into his pocket and dropped a stack of money on the counter.

"What's this?"

"It was in the pocket of your sweatshirt last night. She returned it this morning." Ward's heart stopped for a moment, and he stopped eating, waiting for Ice to continue. "She's different. She insisted that you get every dollar back, because she, and I quote, 'didn't want you to pass by the next person that needed your kindness because you thought they'd steal from you.'"

Ward's gut churned. It was pocket change to him, but it could've helped her. "She should've kept it."

"I agree."

"But you let her return it."

"She insisted. It was important to her. I got her to keep the sweater."

Ward shook his head. "Did you at least get her name? I didn't last night, and I've been kicking myself for it."

"No. I asked. She declined to answer. As I said, she's different."

"Is she still at the hotel?"

"No, the staff said she left the key in the room when she left this morning and hadn't been back."

Ward returned his attention to his dinner, lost in thought. She might be the only woman he'd ever met that had not only not asked him for anything but made sure she hadn't taken anything either. He didn't know what to do with that. All he knew was that it felt good to be with her. She'd been in trouble, and he didn't know where she was or if she was safe.

EIGHT

SYDNEY

It was late as Sydney walked through the ballroom at Keller Event Center for one last check that everything was perfectly set up for the next event. Tables and chairs for 250 guests had to be arranged precisely according to the event schematic. A chunk of Sydney's day had been spent placing them and covering them with matching tablecloths and chair covers. A large section of floor space was left open for dancing, and a small stage was set up for announcements. The bar along the far wall was stocked according to the event plan. Centerpieces took hours to assemble, but they featured photos of smiling children, and Sydney enjoyed looking through them as she put together the intricate arrangements.

It had been a day filled with tasks, but she was the only one assigned to work at Keller for the day, so it was quiet. She had plenty of time to dwell on everything. She was still rattled by Tad's anger. Her mind replayed the assault, and she jumped at small sounds.

She had never felt unsafe before. Overworked, unwanted, invisible, but never unsafe. Her wrist had turned an angry shade of purple, and she kept it wrapped while she worked. The pain was a constant reminder that things had changed. Ice must have seen the bruising when she tried to give Ward's hoodie back, but he hadn't said anything. It didn't matter now. She'd never see him or Ward again. The thought shouldn't leave her feeling desolate, but it did. She was devastated that she'd given away the most precious thing she owned. The only tangible reminder of her father and the life she'd had before he died. The only thing that gave her comfort was the look on Ice's face as he accepted it from her. Reverence. Care. It was safe with him. It was the right thing to do.

The event space was as perfect as it could be for the day. As much as she wanted to stay where she could be alone, she had to get home. If she was lucky, everyone would be asleep when she got there, and maybe they would all ignore the fact that she hadn't come home last night.

Sydney caught the last bus and trudged the rest of the way home, her anxiety increasing with each step. Lights were on in the house. That wasn't a good sign. She stood still, about a block away, staring at the house that once held happy memories. Now, she didn't want to take another step closer.

Ava. She was doing this for Ava. She could do this. One foot in front of the other. Soon, Ava would graduate, and they'd figure out what to do next, but for now, she just had to keep moving forward.

Sydney walked up the front steps and barely opened the door when Belinda grabbed it and jerked it open all the way. "Where have you been?" she shrieked, startling Sydney so badly she stumbled backward onto the porch. Tad grabbed her injured wrist and pulled her inside, slamming the door, ever mindful of what the neighbors might think. Tears sprung to Sydney's eyes at the pressure on her wrist, but she didn't say anything. He squeezed harder.

"Answer her. Where have you been?" he growled in her face.

Sydney didn't know what to say. She didn't have access to money, so admitting she'd been at a hotel was a recipe for disaster. They would want to know where she got the money. They'd probably think she'd stolen it from them.

"I didn't feel comfortable coming home after what happened at Black," she admitted.

Tad's eyes narrowed. "What, exactly, do you think happened?"

She glanced at Belinda and wondered if she knew that Tad was selling more than alcohol. She tried to figure out what to say that was honest but wouldn't get her into more trouble. She finally blurted, "A customer assaulted me. I felt unsafe."

"So you just disappeared overnight?" Belinda yelled, throwing her hands up in the air in exasperation. "You could've been dead, and we didn't know." That could almost be construed as worry for her wellbeing, but Sydney was sure they were more interested in her ability to work for free.

"I'm sorry," she forced herself to mutter. She tried to pull away, but Tad was still much too close and still had a hold of her arm.

"Don't you ever pull something like that again." He lowered his voice. "Or it'll be your precious sister that I'll set up for the next customer."

Sydney jerked back and pulled away, ignoring the stab of pain that shot up her arm. She rushed up the stairs to her room and stopped when she saw the door open. Her room was a disaster. Her blankets were ripped, and the secret floorboard had been pulled up. She whirled around and found Belinda at the bottom of the stairs with a handful of pink envelopes.

"Looking for these?" she called.

"What ..." Sydney couldn't ask why they'd been snooping in her room. They'd always made clear that it was their house.

Belinda turned to the fireplace, and Sydney raced back down the stairs. "No! Please don't!" she called, reaching Belinda just as she tossed the envelopes into the flames.

In seconds, all of her conversations with her sister were gone, as if they had never existed. Sydney dropped to her knees in front of the fireplace, and tears streamed down her cheeks. Those letters were the one thing that she owned and relied on to help her get through the day. The reminders that her sister was counting on her. The silly stories Ava shared about teachers and her school. Any clues she might have had about where she was were gone in a puff of smoke and flame. She'd memorized every word, but now she was terrified she may have forgotten something important, the key clue to finding her.

"Let this be a lesson to you, Sydney. You're here, and your sister's expenses are paid for, because we allow it to be so. Take one more step out of line, and you will regret it for the rest of your life." Belinda whirled around and left the room. Tad remained and watched as Sydney picked herself up and climbed the stairs once more.

Back in her room, Sydney was too tired to put everything back the way it should be. She pulled together as many of her blankets as she could and burrowed in. As she tried to sleep, Tad's words came back to her. He'd sell Ava's body to a customer at Black without hesitation. Shudders racked Sydney's body, and her wrist throbbed. She could still smell the man's breath. Sydney couldn't let that happen to Ava.

The next morning, she wanted to leave for work as early as possible. She willed Belinda and Chantelle to eat faster, tapping her finger on the counter. Even though Chantelle now had a full-time job that she was happy to go to, she still took her time in the mornings.

Belinda stood at the door and snapped, "You're not going to win Ward over enough to be on his arm at the gala this weekend if you don't put in some effort and get there early!" Chantelle jumped up with a dreamy grin on her face and shoved her plate away.

Sydney's stomach turned. Ward? That's who Chantelle was fawning over? She understood it, but the thought of him with Chantelle made her nauseous. He deserved someone who wasn't just after the optics of being with him. She may have only spent a few minutes with him, but he'd been respectful. Thoughtful. Kind. Not at all the arrogant playboy the tabloids made him out to be. She thought back to what Chantelle said about working with him, now that she knew who she'd been gushing about. Looks. All Sydney could remember Chantelle going on about was how attractive he was.

The door slammed as Chantelle and Belinda left for work, and Sydney made quick work of the dishes and rushed out herself. She realized how lucky she'd been that they hadn't seen her when she'd gone to the McKinney building. She had no idea that's where they worked, and it would have been difficult to explain why she was there.

Sydney checked her watch and sighed. She had hoped to have more time before her shift at the diner. She rushed out the door and to the library as quickly as possible. Once there, she only had a few minutes, but she was determined to find Ava, and this was the only place she could think to start.

She started searching private boarding schools and finding their contact information. It was like finding a needle in a haystack, but she couldn't get discouraged.

She closed her eyes and took a deep breath as she signed off from the library computer. With only a few open minutes here and there, she was going to run out of time to find her. And what could she even tell her? She could tell her she loved her, and not to come home. A few tears escaped as she rushed to the diner.

Ward smiled to himself as he read the email from his attorney. Tate was making it too easy to exploit his weaknesses. Ward didn't have anything against the man personally, but he did enjoy making money, and Tate seemed to have good ideas and terrible execution. It would be a crime to let all of that potential go to waste.

As he stepped out of his office, Chantelle stopped him with a hand to his arm. "Do you have a date for the gala tonight?" she asked with hope in her tone.

He shook his head. "I've decided to go solo."

She pouted. "I'd be happy to join you."

He muttered, "You and an army of others," and continued to the elevator. He felt better and better about his decision to go alone. He met up with Ice and headed home to change.

"Why do we do these things again?" Ward asked on the drive to the venue. Ice remained quiet, even though he was usually the one to gripe about evening activities.

He still hadn't said a word as they checked in and walked into the event space. Ice, as usual for these things, drifted off to the side of the room and observed, leaving Ward to mingle on his own. His resolve to be alone wavered for a moment, but he watched the interactions between other wealthy men like him and their trophy girlfriends and cringed.

He'd been to a few events here at Keller Event Center before, but he'd never paid much attention to the venue itself. The floor-to-ceiling windows overlooking the waterfront would give a spectacular view in the daylight. The wood floors could be original to the building, and the exposed beams lent charm to the overall look.

Ward mingled, socialized, and enjoyed the appetizers circulating the room. They were surprisingly tasty, and he found himself reaching for more. Out of the corner of his eye, a wisp of blonde hair caught his attention, and he paused mid-sentence to watch the woman bringing out more trays of food. He excused himself from his conversation and found Ice at his side again as he followed her back into the kitchen where a few workers were busy plating food. He waited until she turned and startled at his presence. He moved in closer.

"Hey, I was hoping to run into you." Not his smoothest opening line, but it was honest.

Her eyes darted around, but no one else in the room seemed to be paying them any attention. The others picked up trays and headed back out.

"Hi," she replied as she made eye contact and took a step back.

"Is everything okay? Are you safe?" It was the question that haunted him since the festival.

Her eyes widened, and she was quick to assure him with a nod, but there was a stiffness in her body language that didn't convince him.

"You need to go, Ward. I can't be seen with you."

That rocked him back on his heels. He grinned. "Everyone wants to be seen with me." It was arrogant but true.

She shook her head and fidgeted with her hair, tucking it behind her ear. "In another lifetime, I'm sure I'd be one of them, enjoying your attention and your kindness. But here, truly, I can't be seen with you. Please go." She moved toward him and tried to usher him to the door. When the door opened and a large man entered the room, she jumped back.

"Sydney! Get more food out there!" he bellowed.

At her wide-eyed fear, Ward pivoted and grabbed a couple of cookies from a platter and addressed the man. "I wanted to compliment the staff. These things are incredible." Ice grabbed a couple as well, and they both made their exit from the kitchen.

"Well, that didn't go quite like I'd hoped," he muttered to Ice. The cookies, though, were indeed amazing.

The MC for the evening called everyone to take their seats for dinner and the fundraising part of the event. Before Ward sat, Ice put a hand on his shoulder.

"Do you know what this organization does?" Ice asked him.

The question made him feel guilty and uncomfortable. He had to shake his head. "Something to help kids." He couldn't get that wrong. There were pictures of kids on the tables.

"You've attended this fundraiser for years. Maybe pay attention this time? This one is important to me. Without New Hope, you wouldn't have the well-adjusted, stable best friend that you have."

"Wait, what?" Ice was already walking away. Ward dropped heavily into his seat and listened for the first time to the stories that were told of New Hope's successes. Moms and kids, given resources and support to exit domestic violence and homeless situations. A safe place for kids to gather. Counseling. Tutoring. Positive role models. All good things, and Ward had no idea that Ice had ever been in a situation to need those services. When it came time for donating, he committed to a hefty amount, but it felt hollow. It was just money. There must be more that he could be doing.

He looked over and realized Chantelle was in attendance after all, wearing a slinky, red dress with a plunging neckline. This was why he enjoyed having Marian as his assistant. She would never show up to a charity gala showing inappropriate amounts of skin. He frowned at her. She was sitting at a table with a woman that looked familiar, but Ward couldn't place her. With the fundraising part of the evening complete, everyone stood to mingle once more and enjoy the desserts that now lined the side tables. Ward met up with Ice, who was swiping more strawberry merengue cookies.

They stood along the wall for a few minutes, watching the buzz of activity. Chantelle made her way over to them and asked Ward to dance. He answered with a curt, "No," and she moved on with a pout, swaying her hips more than necessary as she walked away. "What's she doing here?" he wondered aloud.

"No idea, but she was talking with Belinda from HR during the presentation. Maybe they came together."

"On whose dime?" Maybe he was being pretentious, but this was an expensive event to attend, and she was an assistant. "I'm sorry I hadn't been paying attention. I didn't know this organization was important to you."

Ice shrugged. "Elementary school, before I knew you. Thanks for taking it seriously now."

Ward sipped from a glass of water. "I want to do something more than throw money at them."

Ice nodded. "I'm sure there's something you can get your fingers into."

Sydney appeared in front of them with a tray in hand. "Can I talk to you for a minute?"

Mindful of the room full of people, Ward nodded rather than letting it show that he wanted nothing more than to give her his full attention. Ice put a hand out to stop him from following her directly. After she disappeared into the kitchen, Ice followed, and then Ward followed them both. Ice opened a door, letting him into a small room with her, little more than a closet. Ward approached her once more, stepping into her personal space. He felt drawn to her like a magnet, a pull deep in his chest.

She raised a hand as he got too close. "I wanted to warn you to be careful what you say around your assistant." Ward's body tensed, and his eyes narrowed. "She's probably as shallow as she seems, but she also seems naive enough that she doesn't realize when someone is prodding her for information that she shouldn't share."

"How do you know who my assistant is?"

Sydney rolled her eyes. "No one notices the wait staff at these things. People just talk as if we're not here."

After a pause, Ward said, "Thanks for the warning." He moved a bit closer and slowly brought a hand up to cup her cheek. She leaned into his touch, emboldening him to ask in a hushed voice, "Can I kiss you?" It was dumb. He barely knew her, but he wanted to. He stopped breathing, afraid he'd scared her off.

Instead of pushing him away, though, she just shook her head. She slipped her arms under his jacket and wrapped them around him tightly. She pressed her face to his neck, her breath shaky at first. He returned the embrace, and they stood there for a long moment. The innocence and comfort she brought him with one hug left him simultaneously fulfilled and craving more.

When she stepped back, she smoothed her hair and smiled. "I'm going to have a difficult enough time making sure it doesn't look like I just spent time alone with Seattle's most eligible bachelor. Thank you for the hug, Ward. I needed it." She slipped out of the room before he could reply.

It took him a full minute to pull himself together.

Who knew that a simple hug would undo him? Ice tapped on the door and opened it. "We need to get back out there. You okay?"

Ward nodded and followed him back out into the social chaos. Other business leaders stopped him to chat. Women stopped him to ask to dance. All Ward could think about was that nothing in this room mattered. There were children out there that needed help. Ice had needed help when he was young. Sydney needed help and hadn't asked for any. She hadn't asked for anything at all. In the short time that he'd known her, she'd only given him peace. Even as he worried about her, thinking about her gave him peace. He was having a bit of a crisis, realizing just how self-absorbed he'd been.

He ignored Chantelle's approach once more and spent some time talking with the director of New Hope. He made sure to get her information to follow up and find out what more he could do.

An idea was starting to come together, and he scanned the crowd. He hadn't seen Robert Tate at this event. Robert's financial situation wouldn't allow him to be here, but it was one of the business community's major events of the year, and it could be seen as a scandal that he was missing.

Satisfied that he'd done what he came to do, Ward grabbed his outerwear from coat check and stepped outside into the frosty air. He stood there, watching his breath puff into the air, while Ice shrugged into his coat.

"Everything okay? It's not like you to leave a party early."

He let the question hang in the air. "I'm an idiot. And I don't think I want to be one anymore."

Ice laughed. "Okay, Ward. Anything I can help with?" he asked as they headed to the car.

Ward paused and detoured to walk along the waterfront park. "I want to know more about Sydney. See what you can find out. And I want to get rid of Chantelle. I know I can't, but I can spend more time working from home. I don't trust her, and Sydney overheard her answering questions about working for me, what I'm working on."

"I'll make some inquiries. Chantelle was talking to HR. Maybe she just overheard shop talk."

Ward shook his head. "Maybe, but her point was that Chantelle is the type to answer questions without considering the consequences. I don't trust her with what I'm working on." He watched a bird land on a bench and take off again on the breeze. "Why didn't you tell me about New Hope earlier?"

Ice was silent for a few beats. "It was before we met. I don't like to talk about that time in my life, though everyone at New Hope was wonderful. I kept hoping that you'd eventually hear their message. Better late than never, my friend." He slapped Ward on the back, and they turned back toward the car.

TEN

SYDNEY

The next several days were grueling. Sydney reset the event space for the anniversary celebration that would be held the next weekend. She was scheduled at the diner early every morning, the event space for an hour or two, and then Black, every day. She was barely getting any sleep, much less making any progress on finding Ava.

Over breakfast each morning, she had to listen to Chantelle go on and on about how wonderful Ward was. It was the only time Sydney had ever felt jealous of Chantelle. Sydney wanted to see him again, to hug him again, and she knew it wasn't likely to ever happen. The memory of being in his arms would have to be enough.

Her shifts at Black had her on edge. She was extra careful to stick to the dishes and the cleaning that kept her away from the hallway and away from Tad. She couldn't avoid him completely, and she was confused by his behavior when they did cross paths. He acted like nothing was wrong, like he wasn't doing anything shady.

The more he acted like everything was fine, the more she wanted to know what he was up to. Maybe if Black was closed down for illegal activities, she'd get some freedom back. She dismissed that thought almost as quickly as it appeared, but she was determined to keep her eyes and ears open.

Saturday night, Sydney found herself working the anniversary party for the city's mayor and his wife at the event center. Tad was more overbearing than usual for this event, hoping to impress the mayor. He'd been hovering all afternoon as food was prepared and plated. He adjusted Sydney's hairband before he allowed her out amongst the guests with trays of food.

The guests were having a good time, toasting the presumably happy couple, dancing, and drinking. As the event wound down and Sydney was cleaning up in the kitchen alone, she heard the door open and stiffened, expecting Tad to start criticizing something she had done.

When that didn't happen, she glanced up and was surprised to find Ward beside her, his hands in his pockets. Her gaze flew to the doorway in alarm, and her heart raced. "You can't be here," she whispered.

"Ice is watching the door. We have a couple of minutes," he assured her.

"What are you even doing here? You weren't on the guest list." She had hand-lettered all of the place cards for the event. She would've remembered writing his name.

Ward shrugged. "No one even blinked when I walked in. I needed to see you. What's your real name?"

Sydney frowned. "What do you mean? You overheard it at the gala. Sydney. Sydney Harrett."

He shook his head and came closer. "See, that's where there's some confusion." He stood so close, she could feel his breath on her cheek, and he dropped his voice to a near whisper. "There isn't a Sydney on the payroll for this event center. So I looked up the owner, and you don't seem to work for any of the companies with shared ownership."

"Yet, here I am," she whispered back.

He glanced back at the door. "I know we don't have much time. Agree to meet me somewhere. Anywhere that we can talk."

"I can't do that," she insisted, closing her eyes and imagining for a moment that it was possible. That she could spend more time with this man who, inexplicably, seemed to care about her.

He studied her. "We won't be seen. Anywhere you want. Any time. Please, Sydney. I have questions that I can't ask you here."

"My time is not my own."

He considered that. "Surely you have to get from place to place. Let us drive you."

He was still so close that Sydney dropped her forehead to his chest for just a moment, taking a deep breath. When she straightened, she said, "Tomorrow, I'm supposed to be at the diner until one, and then I have to be at Black by two. I need to go to the library in between. It's important."

"If we drive, you'll have more time there."

"Okay, but no one can know, Ward."

"I know," he promised, dropping a light kiss to her hair before stepping back. "I'll see you tomorrow."

He crossed the room and cautiously left. Sydney covered her racing heart with her hand. She forced herself to focus on the task at hand. She couldn't be caught slacking off now. She couldn't give Tad any reason to change her schedule. As she finished cleaning up, Sydney realized the implications of what Ward said. He'd somehow pulled employment records for Tad's companies. She didn't even know that was possible. She hoped Tad wouldn't find out.

Sydney was on edge the rest of the night, jumping at any small sound. She was anxious about being caught talking to Ward. What would she even have to talk with him about? Why did he care? He'd gone out of his way to see her, and she just couldn't understand it.

As she made breakfast the next morning, Sydney had a new fear. What if Chantelle knew what Ward was doing? What if she had been asked to make the inquiries? She was relieved by the normalcy of the morning as Chantelle and Belinda appeared, ate, and left.

She was still on edge catching the bus to the diner. She couldn't stop the tremor that continued to run through her body throughout the morning. While she was completing her cleaning tasks, someone startled her, and she whirled around, her hand flying to her chest.

"I'm so sorry to startle you, Sydney," one of the waitresses, Leah, soothed. "I just wanted to check and see if you were okay. You've been a little jumpy today."

Sydney's heart rate settled, and she smiled to reassure her. "I'm fine, thanks Leah."

She wasn't easily convinced. "You're sure? If you need to talk or anything ..."

Sydney realized her wrist was still discolored and figured that might be triggering some of the concern. It was nice to have someone ask, but there was no way she was bringing Leah into this. "Really, thank you for asking. I really appreciate it."

Leah nodded and returned to the dining room. Sydney finished up, grabbed Ward's hoodie from the breakroom, and pulled it over her head. She left the diner and breathed in the cool afternoon air. She wondered if Ward was going to show up and how he planned to do so without being obvious. She didn't have to wonder for long.

A block from the diner, around the corner from the door, Ward stepped out of a doorway and walked alongside her, veering them into the next side street and opening a car door for her. She got in without question, and he got in on the other side. Ice was at the wheel.

"Hi," she greeted Ice as she put on her seatbelt.

"Good afternoon, Sydney," he replied, putting the car in gear as soon as Ward was in.

Ward put his hand, palm up, on the seat between them, inviting but not assuming that his touch would be welcome. Sydney only hesitated for a moment before putting her hand in his. She hadn't realized how cold her hands were until she felt the warmth of Ward's.

"Hi, Sydney," he finally greeted her.

"Hi," she replied simply, focused on their joined hands. The steady, gentle pressure of Ward's thumb against her hand was comforting, and Sydney wished this moment was a normal one in her life. What she wouldn't give for a stable, healthy relationship with someone who could take care of themselves and those around them.

"Why are we going to the library?" he asked as they pulled into the parking lot.

She closed her eyes. She didn't want to go through this with him. She didn't want to open her life up to him. "It's a long story," she replied, hoping to put him off. She unbuckled her seat belt, but she didn't let go of his hand yet.

"You don't owe me any personal information, Sydney. I hope you don't feel obligated. But I care about you. I want to help. I'm concerned about your safety. Can you at least tell me if you're safe?"

She thought about that and chose honesty. "I think so. Nothing else has happened that sent me running into the streets at night." She smiled, hoping for some levity, but Ward's expression remained grim.

"I'd like to hear the rest of the story from that night at some point."

Sydney pulled away and opened the door, stepping out and walking to the library. The car doors thudded shut, and Ward and Ice were right behind her. She went straight to the computers but quickly realized that they couldn't talk out in public. Perhaps that worked in her favor, as she didn't want to share, but she also recognized that they had taken time out of their day to be here, to pick her up, to drive her to Black. She turned back and waited while Ward caught up with her. Ice hung back, giving them privacy.

Sydney blew out a breath. "Why?" she asked as Ward reached her.

"Why what?" he asked with genuine confusion.

"Why are you being kind to me? Why are you here?"

Ward leaned closer and brushed a lock of hair from her face. "You are the only person who thinks I'm kind."

She stared at him. "I don't think that's an answer."

He chuckled. "I suppose you're right. It's true, though. I don't know what it is about you that brings that out of me. I care, Sydney. I've seen you afraid, yet you're so strong. I don't know what you're facing, but I'm a pretty good problem solver. It's what I do. And if there's anything I can do to help you, even if it's just to listen, I want to be here."

She blinked back tears at his sincerity. She took his hand and led him over to a small meeting room. Ice paused at the doorway, as if to just stand guard, but she waved him in. "If I'm going to share anything, you may as well both be in the room. If you don't mind, that is," she rushed to add, realizing it was presumptuous to think he'd care.

Ice closed the door as he entered and nodded to her.

"One thing, before I say anything else. You said I wasn't on the employee lists for the restaurants. How do you know that?"

Ward and Ice looked at each other. "I have contacts," Ward answered. "They find me information on all sorts of projects I'm working on. Various financial information, including payroll data sometimes."

"Does your assistant know you were asking around about this? About me?" Sydney couldn't stop the tremor in her voice.

"No. What do you know about Chantelle that we don't, Sydney?" Ward took her hand, and they sat around the small table with Ice closest to the door.

"It's complicated. She's my stepsister. If she finds out I even know you, she'll be quick to share that information with her mom, who got her the job, and with Tad."

Ice's eyebrow lifted. "Belinda is Chantelle's mom?" He made the connection quickly.

Sydney nodded. "I meant what I said at the gala. Chantelle is fine. She's just not good at nuance or filtering herself, and for you, I'm concerned that she would just spill anything to anyone who asks."

"I appreciate that. What's the connection between Belinda and restauranteur Tad?"

"Belinda married him after my dad died."

Ice's finger tapped the table in a steady rhythm, and he kept his eyes on the door, but he nodded.

Ward leaned forward in his chair, still holding Sydney's hand. He asked, "Why are you working off the books in Tad's businesses? What do they have over you, Syd?"

Sydney took a deep breath. His concern was just too much, and a tear slipped down her cheek. Ward lightly swept it away. "My little sister. My wages pay for her boarding school."

Ward and Ice both nodded, but it wasn't enough. Before he could ask the follow-up questions that she could see formulating behind his stormy eyes, she added, "Belinda moved her to boarding school shortly after she married Tad. I don't know where she is, Ward." Two sets of eyes snapped to focus on her. "We write letters to each other, but I receive them in a blank envelope, and Belinda mails mine. They've never once allowed me to see a piece of information on where she is. I have to find her before graduation this spring. I've been researching schools," she gestured out to the library.

Ward abruptly stood and pulled Sydney into a hug, and the floodgates opened. She couldn't control the tears, and Ward just held her tighter as she cried.

Ice's voice broke through. "What's her name, Sydney?"

She looked over at him and tried to pull herself together. "Ava Harrett, but I don't even know if that's what last name she's using. It should be, it's our father's, but what if they enrolled her with Tad's last name?" She shuddered.

"We'll find her, Syd. Just do what you have to do until then, but we'll find her. Trust us?"

She nodded and stepped back, wiping her face. "Sorry for all of the drama." Both men chuckled, startling her.

Ward squeezed her hand. "That wasn't drama. We've seen drama. Thank you for trusting us with this. I know there's more, but we need to get you to your next gig."

"Wait." Ice held up his hand. "You don't have to go.

What's stopping you from quitting, just walking away? You'd have more time to search for her, and when you found her, you could catch up any missed tuition, if there was any. The term is probably already paid for. I'm missing part of the picture, and it seems important."

He was sharp. Too sharp. She cleared her throat. "They've threatened to pull her out of school if I step out of line. Then she'd be stuck doing the same thing I am, working under Tad's thumb all day, every day. And ..." She swallowed hard. "I just found out there are some shady things going on at Black. I'm usually in the back, washing dishes, out of the way, and didn't know ... but I don't want Ava there. She's turning eighteen. She has her life ahead of her. I want good things for her. And being stuck at Black? Possibly being forced or persuaded to allow customers to touch her?" She shook her head and blinked back more tears. She had cried enough in front of these two patient men. "I need to go," she choked out.

Ward pulled her back in and held her for another long moment. Before they left the room, Ice pulled her into a brief hug as well. "We've got this, Sydney," he murmured, gesturing for her to leave the room first. She took a deep breath before heading back through the library to the front door. They were right behind her, and all were silent for the few-minute drive to Black.

"If you're unsafe, Sydney, leave. You know where to find me, and here's my number." He handed her his card with his personal number and Ice's written across the back. "We'll figure it out, okay?"

"Thanks for listening. Both of you. This isn't your

problem, and I shouldn't have dumped it on you, but I appreciate your time and concern."

"It's what friends do, Syd."

Ice parked the car a few blocks from Black, and she jumped out, thankful for the rush of cool air that calmed her overheated skin. The tears had dried, and she hoped she looked presentable as she dashed into the restaurant and clocked in right on time.

Ice didn't move to start the car after Sydney got out. Ward moved up to the passenger seat, and they both sat in silence.

Ice cleared his throat and flexed his fingers on the steering wheel. "How the hell are we supposed to find her sister? It's not like we can just call the schools and ask if she's registered there. They aren't going to release that information."

Ward leaned his head back and closed his eyes. "I don't know. I should've asked Sydney how she was planning to find her. I don't think claiming to be her sister would help."

"Are we checking out Black tonight?"

Ward tensed. "I don't know."

Ice turned and stared at him. "Why not? You get your 'going out' fix and see what's up, win win."

Ward looked out the window at the steady stream of cars going by and thought through his reaction. "If there's something going on, I'm not sure I want to know. I don't know that I could walk out of there without her."

Ice started the car and drove them back to the office. Before he turned off the engine, he turned back to Ward. "She's put up with this for who knows how long. She'll be okay until we can figure this out. For now, you need to keep Chantelle busy enough that she doesn't realize you aren't giving her any real work to do."

Ward smiled as an idea came to him. "I think she'd be excellent at planning an anniversary party for Dad and Lisa."

"I think your dad would have a heart attack if you suddenly approved of his wife."

Guilt hit Ward hard. "I've been awful to her, and she's never been anything but nice to me. I should make it right. We know Chantelle has the connections to make an event happen, and Sydney would most likely be working it, based on the last two events we attended at Keller. I don't see a downside."

Ice shrugged and turned off the engine, and they both got out of the car. "You'll be able to hold it together?" he asked.

Ward nodded. "I'll text you if I need to bail. And I'll think about Black."

They walked into the building and went their separate ways. When he stepped off the elevator, Chantelle quickly brushed something into her desk drawer. She blew on her fingers as if her nails were drying. Ward shook his head. The company was paying his assistant to do her nails. Fantastic.

"You're back!" she exclaimed, rising and waving her nails in the air. "You didn't have anything on your calendar, and I didn't know where you went. Is everything okay?" She followed him into his office. "Do you need anything?"

Ward took a deep breath. "I'm fine. I had lunch with Ice." It was close enough to the truth. They did grab a light lunch before picking up Sydney, and he was glad they hadn't eaten anything heavier. "I actually do have a project for you. After your nails dry."

She blushed. "The phones have been quiet. I'll get my notepad, and you can tell me all about this project." She backed out of the room and was back in moments.

She sat in the chair across from him. Ward searched his calendar for his dad's wedding date. He was sure their anniversary was coming up, but he had blocked the date from his memory. He'd still been so bitter about his mom leaving when he was a teenager that he'd refused to believe Lisa would stick around. They'd been married five years already, and Ward hadn't given her a break for a second. He was finally feeling the shame in that. There it was, March 31, just a few weeks away. Perfect. It even fell on a weekend this year.

"How are you at event planning?" he asked, knowing full well that she'd excel at it.

Chantelle perked up in her chair, and a huge smile spread across her face. "I love planning special events! What is the occasion?"

"I'd like to throw a surprise anniversary party for my father and his wife, Lisa. Their anniversary is March 31.

I trust that will be enough time to pull something together. I'm sure his assistant will have some insight into who should be on the guest list."

She was literally bouncing in her chair, writing furiously on her notepad. This was the most interested Chantelle had been in her job since she started. "It will be the event of the year!" she exclaimed.

Ward sat back and watched as she jumped up and rushed back to her desk to start putting things in motion. She popped her head back in almost immediately. "Do you think the Keller Event Center will be okay? I know the owner and think I can get you a deal."

Ward swallowed the bile that threatened to rise at the thought of giving any money to a man that had Sydney trapped in a life of labor. He forced a smile and replied, "It seems to be the venue of the season. It will be fine. Thanks, Chantelle."

Once she was happily busy, Ward closed his door and tried to return his thoughts to work. Paperwork had come through from his attorney on the property near the one Tate wanted for his project. Ward was determined to put something there that would both thwart Tate's efforts and make McKinney Enterprises a lot of money. Now he also thought he might be able to include a resource center for New Hope in the plans. This could be his pinnacle project.

The next few hours flew by as Ward buried himself in details for the new project. He spent an hour meeting with his favorite architect to design something that would overshadow whatever Tate was dreaming about. If he could get the permits applied for first, he was confident his contractors could pull the project off before Tate even knew what was happening. The arrogance of that man to think only his company could manage a project like this. What did he think Ward did all day?

When Ice appeared in his office, Ward was feeling pretty good, like he could conquer the world.

"Your assistant is gone for the day already."

Ward checked the time. That was unusual. She'd been hanging around, usually trying to wait to leave until Ward left, and he'd had to shoo her out of the office. He shrugged. "She was more excited than I expected with her new project. Hopefully it'll keep her busy for a while."

As they left the building, Ice waited before pulling out. Ward knew what he was asking without words. "Yeah, okay, let's check it out. One drink."

Ice didn't comment; he just put the car in gear and navigated to the trendy restaurant. There had been some buzz when it opened, but Ward hadn't been, preferring to stick to restaurants he had history with, especially for business meetings. After hours, he preferred loud clubs over venues like this that were more about drinking and socializing.

When they arrived, they were quickly seated at a tall, round table that had barely enough surface area for any food to be served. Both glanced through the menu and closed it pretty quickly. The food seemed to be standard bar fare dressed up to sound pretentious.

Their server arrived, dressed in a black button-down

shirt with three-quarter sleeves like the one Sydney always wore. Unlike Sydney, though, the first several buttons were left open, and she paired it with an excessively short black skirt. She gave them a flirtatious smile. "What can I get you fine gentlemen this evening?"

They both ordered club sodas and "Distressed Snap Peas and Seasoned Croquets" with zero expectations.

Their server hinted heavily that they were missing out by skipping the alcohol, but neither caved. The last thing Ward wanted to feel here was out of control. He tried to relax, but the stools were hard and an awkward height. This was not a place that invited you to stay and drink for long periods, which wouldn't be possible for most people at their prices anyway.

The money wasn't an issue for Ward, of course, but he still bristled at supporting Tad in any way. The club sodas arrived quickly, and they were left to wait for their food, giving them plenty of time for people watching. The place was fairly busy for a weeknight, and most of the patrons were younger men in their twenties and thirties. Ward and Ice fit in, but Ward felt old amidst the preening crowd. These were the types in suits with slicked back hair, puffed up chests, and superiority complexes.

He looked over at Ice. "Does this place make you feel as old as it makes me feel?"

Ice laughed. "You? Feel old? You're the one that still goes clubbing. *This* place makes you feel old?"

Ward could see the humor in it. "Yes. One hundred percent." He tried not to react as their server brought out their food and leaned close to suggest he might enjoy it more with a nice Reisling. The dish looked a little sad, which he expected. The tiny, bright yellow plate held half a dozen sauteed snap peas and four of the smallest croquettes he'd ever seen.

When the server didn't back away, Ward glared at her until she got the message. She finally moved on, tossing Ice a flirty smile. Ward picked at his food and found it as tasteless as it looked. So far, the only thing he'd seen was obnoxious clientele and flirty waitresses, which was pretty normal for any drinking establishment. Ice excused himself, and Ward pulled out his phone. He found a lengthy email from Chantelle, detailing her plans so far. This project wasn't going to take her anywhere near as long as it needed to.

He was focused on an email from his architect when Ice returned and didn't sit. He stood fidgeting, which was strange for him. He gestured for their server and asked for the check. Ward stood and scanned the room again, wondering what had Ice so worked up. They waited too long for the check, and Ward tossed cash on the table.

They walked out, and instead of turning toward the car, Ice turned the other way. They walked a few blocks, and Ice pushed into a club that Ward frequented. He walked up to the bar, ordered two shots of tequila and downed them both before Ward even caught up. Ward pulled him over to a table, away from the chaos of the dance floor. It was too loud to talk, which left Ward frustrated and twitchy. Ice was the calm one, always in control.

He was still in control, but his emotions weren't locked down. He couldn't stand still, and his facial expressions ranged from anger to anguish. Ward had never seen him like this. He walked over to the bar and came back with another shot for Ice and two club sodas.

Ice nodded when they finished their drinks, and they walked back out into the cold. Ice handed over his keys, and Ward drove them home on autopilot. It was convenient living in the same building. Ice followed him up to his condo and flopped down in one of the recliners in Ward's living room.

Ice pulled a hand down his face and blew out a breath. "I went down the hallway to find the restroom and to see what the rest of the place was like. I wish I hadn't. The bartender on that side was openly selling drugs to multiple customers. Another employee was up against the wall being felt up by a customer."

"You're sure it was an employee?"

Ice nodded. "Same uniform, and she didn't seem into it but wasn't pushing him away. Didn't seem like a boyfriend. And he was asking her to take him to the back room. That he'd make it worth her while. I don't like it."

Ward was glad it'd been Ice and not him that had seen firsthand that Sydney was right, that illegal things were happening, and happening in plain sight. "You were the one calmly assuring me that Sydney was going to be fine. Don't change your mind now."

A moment of silence passed. "I still think she'll hang in there as long as she needs to. But hasn't she been through enough?"

Ward agreed but had to lighten the mood. "Am I going to have to fight you for her once she's clear of all this?"

His words had the intended effect. Ice laughed. "I like her, but not like that. You're the one that pulled her from thin air." His hand drifted to his neckline, and he pulled out a chain, pulling it over his head. "I don't think I told you about this, though, and I should." He passed the chain with a ring attached over to Ward.

"What's this?" Ward asked quietly, running his finger over the delicate design carved into the wide but feminine silver band.

"It's Sydney's. The same day she brought your money back, she asked me to keep it safe for her, even though she didn't think she'd ever see it again. She said she couldn't keep it safe anymore. Her dad designed it and gave it to her before he died. I am determined to make sure she gets it back as soon as she's in a safe, stable place. She trusted me with this, Ward. She didn't know me. I'll do anything I can to help her."

After a deep breath, he added, "And I like her for you. It's like she flipped a switch when you pulled her out of that crowd, and you're different. You're throwing your dad an anniversary party, and I heard you say Lisa's name without disdain. I haven't had to get you through a group of paparazzi in days." He smiled.

Ward was still mesmerized by the ring. It was beautiful, crafted with love. It hadn't escaped him that if she'd handed it off to a virtual stranger, things were bad at home. He handed it back to Ice, who pulled it back around his neck, tucking it under his shirt. He stood and gave a half wave. "I'm going to go crash. I'll regret the tequila in the morning."

Ward chuckled. "An extra mile on our run in the morning, then?"

Ice flipped him off on the way out the door. The smile stayed on Ward's face for a minute, but it was short-lived. He hated that he couldn't call or text Sydney and check in on her. What kind of monsters threw one child away in boarding school and forced and manipulated the other to work? He forced himself to get ready for bed but lay there for hours, his brain too busy to rest.

Sydney was so tired. She hadn't had a spare moment to herself in days. She hadn't seen Ward or Ice. She didn't know why Tad was making her schedule more and more difficult, but she was at the end of her rope. Her shifts had been so close together, she hadn't gotten to the library. She could only hope that Ward and Ice had ideas and could find Ava. Their words that "it's what friends do" were words she leaned on when she had a moment to think. The idea that she had friends that she could actually rely on was foreign to her.

She walked into the Keller building at 5:30 in the morning, bleary eyed and uncoordinated. Tad informed her when she'd left Black at midnight that there was a two-day business conference starting this morning, and she was responsible for everything. Everything. She groaned and prayed that he hadn't actually meant that the way it sounded.

Once in the building, she left most of the lights off

and headed to the office. The instructions for the event were printed and compiled in a binder on the desk, and she took it to the kitchen to flip through it. A hundred attendees. Two days. Three meals plus snacks each day and beverage service. Tables and chairs in a classroom configuration. Staff list? Just Sydney. She closed her eyes and took a ragged breath. She could do this.

The menu said fresh cinnamon rolls, coffee, and fresh fruit for breakfast. She started the first batch of coffee to get herself jump started and pulled out the cinnamon roll dough, which thankfully had been pre-prepared by the diner's staff. Those went into the oven, and she made quick work of cutting up fresh fruit. With breakfast underway, she flipped on the lights in the main space and pulled out the carts of chairs and arranged thirty tables, rushing back into the kitchen to swap pans of cinnamon rolls in and out of the ovens.

There were supposed to be blue tablecloths on all of the tables, but there was no time to find them, iron them, and lay them out. She set up the podium and AV equipment as the binder dictated. At 7:30, a representative running the conference pounded on the door, startling Sydney. She rushed to open the door and unlocked it. The woman standing there looked harried, her hair windblown and a large box slipping from her grip. Sydney helped her bring it in and saw two more on the ground beside the door. Between the two of them, they got everything inside and placed at a table at the entry for signing in.

"I'm Hannah," she said. "You are?"

Sydney bristled at her haughty tone, hoping that she'd be working with someone reasonable today. "Sydney. Excuse me, I need to get food out of the oven. I'll be back." She got back to the oven just in time and pulled out the last batch. She started another pot of coffee and began arranging breakfast to be ready to go out as soon as attendees started arriving.

"Sydney!" Hannah called loudly.

Sydney wiped her hands on a towel and peeked out of the kitchen. Hannah was still standing where she left her, boxes still unopened on the table. "Yes?" Sydney prompted as she approached.

Hannah looked her up and down. She had fixed her hair and hung her jacket up somewhere and looked put together in a way that Sydney could only dream to achieve. "The sign-in desk needs to be set up, and attendees will arrive soon. You aren't planning on greeting them like that, are you?" She flicked a finger up and down at Sydney.

Sydney blinked at her. "Are you saying that you don't have a representative to sign in your attendees? I'm sorry, that wasn't part of the agreement. I can either assist out here, or I can make sure meals will be prepared and served on time. The schedule is very tight today."

Hannah scowled. "It isn't my problem that you don't have help." She whirled away and walked across the room and out into the hallway.

Sydney had no idea what to do. If she was lucky, Tad could send someone over to help her, but she wasn't allowed to ask, and no one else was on the instruction sheet. She shrugged and unpacked the boxes, which contained packets, presumably for each attendee. One of the boxes contained nametags. She laid everything out as quickly and neatly as possible and then rushed back to the kitchen. Attendees would be arriving any minute, so she brought breakfast out, setting it up on side tables. She could hear people arriving as she returned to the kitchen, and she had to ignore them.

She took a look at the lunch menu and wanted to cry. The amount of preparation required for the lunch and dinner menus was unreasonable for one person. She went through the fridge and freezer, and thankfully, all ingredients appeared to be available, and some things were packaged in a way that made her life a little bit easier, but it was still going to be a challenge.

The sound of heels clacking on the floor grew louder, and Sydney looked up to see Hannah, a deep frown on her face. "I thought I was clear. You are needed to check in attendees. And the speaker is here and ready for his microphone."

Sydney once again blinked at her. "I think there has been a misunderstanding. Our paperwork says that you will be staffing the event. I am here for catering, and I need to get preparation underway for the meals that were ordered. I would help you if I could clone myself, but I wasn't blessed with that ability." Sydney couldn't believe she'd just spoken to a customer that way, but her internal filter had worn away in her weariness. She couldn't take it back.

Hannah huffed and threw her hands up in the air,

spinning on her heel and leaving the kitchen, much to Sydney's relief. It was short lived. The phone in the kitchen rang moments later.

"Yes?" she answered. This wasn't a published number. It could only be one person on the other end of the line.

"Why am I hearing that you aren't fulfilling your duties?" Tad roared through the phone.

"I am the only one scheduled here today, and the instructions say I am responsible for catering. I've completed the room setup and prepared and served breakfast. The meals they've chosen will take the rest of the day to prepare and serve. If I go out there and help with check-in and AV and who knows what else, I won't be able to get the meals out. I can either upset her, or I can upset a hundred attendees. If you can spare someone to help—"

He cut her off. "This is your assignment for the day. Figure it out. Keep the client happy." He hung up.

Hannah was back in the doorway, a smug smile on her face. Sydney approached her and whirled the binder around on the counter to face her. "Here's the deal, Hannah. I want to help you. But if you need my help out there, something is going to have to give. Lunch is going to have to get simpler. I can help you and," she stepped back and opened the fridge, scanning the contents, "we can do sandwiches, or I stay in the kitchen, and we can do the full buffet that was requested."

"Fine. Sandwiches. Come on," Hannah urged.

"Wait. One more thing. Once everyone is checked in

and presentations have started, I need to start work on the dinner buffet entrees as well. I can't get pulled out to other things. We can't do sandwiches again for dinner."

Hannah tapped a perfectly manicured nail against her lips. "Fine." She swept her arm out, stopping Sydney. "The apron stays in the kitchen," she insisted.

Sydney tossed it on the counter and straightened her standard black button-down uniform shirt and followed Hannah back out. She met the speaker and made sure he was all set with his microphone, and she did a quick sound check with him. She was glad that people were enjoying their breakfast.

She made her way back to the sign-in table and took a seat, greeting people and giving them their name badges and packets. She had no idea what this conference was about. Generic business speak garnished the cover of each packet. Everyone arriving was dressed in their business suits, looking like they were ready for the business deal of a lifetime.

Sydney couldn't help but think of Ward as she greeted suit after suit. She overheard snippets of conversations, mostly boasting about their most recent deals, or deals they were on the cusp of closing. The room was filling with a buzz of chatter and energy. Sydney wished she had managed to drink more than a half a cup of coffee.

At nine o'clock on the dot, the presenter kicked off the program to a loud squeal of feedback, and Sydney leaped up from her seat and rushed to the sound board, making the necessary corrections. This was not her forte.

Give her a kitchen, dishes, food, or a mop. She'd never signed up for this.

As soon as the presenter was successfully speaking at a reasonable volume, Sydney escaped to the kitchen. She spent an extra minute with her hands under the hot running water, trying to warm them. She thought she might be freezing due to a lack of sleep, but she also hadn't eaten anything. She pulled out the cinnamon roll she'd set aside for herself and stuffed a piece in her mouth as she pulled out the two meats that needed to roast for most of the day for dinner. She followed the recipes carefully and set the timers. At least that portion of the day's meals was pretty easy, just time consuming.

She pulled together the ingredients for the potatoes au gratin on the dinner menu and worked through that prep methodically, washing and slicing seemingly endless potatoes. Before she knew it, she had to pull the sandwiches together. The fridge contained a good assortment of deli meats and cheeses, as well as lettuce, tomatoes, and onions, and different breads. She made quick work of making sandwiches and found a stash of cookies in the freezer and chips in the pantry. She'd serve the sandwiches and chips with sodas for lunch, and the cookies would be thawed in time for their midafternoon break.

Sydney stood at the doorway, listening for a moment, trying to gauge how close the group was to breaking for lunch. The presenter abruptly released the group, and Sydney rushed to bring the food out. Some attendees headed outside to smoke or get fresh air. Others rushed to the tables as if afraid they would run out of food. Still others were content to remain in conversation at their tables. As far as she knew, no one was angry with her yet, so that was a good sign. She overheard a few grumbles about sandwiches for lunch, but she'd done the best she could, and they looked good.

She wished for a moment of rest, but the dinner preparations called to her. If she hurried, she could get a batch of the strawberry merengues started. That Ward and Ice had enjoyed them meant a lot to her. She knew that Ward had come up with his compliment on the fly to distract Tad, but Ice's smile and wink as he'd taken more had been genuine.

With dinner preparations underway, Sydney was focused on the task at hand when footsteps tapped on the kitchen floor. She sighed, expecting Hannah to be back with more complaints.

"Excuse me, are you Sydney?" the petite woman in a suit and chunky heels asked.

She tried to keep the weariness out of her voice when she replied, "Yes, can I help you?"

She approached, started to hold out her hand, but pulled it back when she noticed Sydney's hands were covered in the dough she was kneading. "My name is Elle, and I'm here to help you."

Sydney frowned at her and shook her head. "I think there's some confusion. You can't be here to help. Tad wouldn't have sent anyone, and you're in a suit."

Elle sidled a little bit closer and dropped her voice. "The suit was a cover to walk in the door without being noticed. My husband Rick is still out there pretending to belong, but he's here to help too. Oliver is my brother."

"I'm still confused. I don't know anyone named Oliver."

Elle laughed. "Right, you probably know him as Ice. Ridiculous name."

Sydney joined her laughter, and an exhausted tear escaped down her cheek. "Ice sent you?" she asked over the lump in her throat. Sydney was overcome and had to stop and pull herself together.

Elle watched her with concern. "What can I do to help?"

"You're serious." It wasn't a question, it was a realization.

"Absolutely. Put me to work. I even know my way around a kitchen. Rick doesn't, but he can carry stuff," she shared with a laugh. She pulled her hair back with a hair tie that she had in her bag, and she hung her bag on a hook. She pulled on an apron and washed her hands.

Sydney pulled the binder over and pulled out the recipe for the salad and handed it over. "If you've got this, the meats are roasting, and the potatoes are in the oven. I was just making some extra desserts." In minutes, Elle was focused, chopping kale and other veggies into the massive salad bowl that Sydney pulled out. Sydney still wasn't sure why Elle was here, but she didn't know how to ask without sounding ungrateful. She'd never been more grateful for someone's actions in her entire life.

They worked well together, finishing the preparations for the meal. Rick helped them move everything out to the buffet tables. As everyone started dishing up their meals, Hannah reappeared at Sydney's side.

"Where is the alcohol?" she asked with an edge to her voice.

Sydney tried to ignore her for a minute, instead watching everyone talking as they piled their plates high.

"Sydney!" Hannah snapped. "The alcohol! There is supposed to be an open bar."

Sydney had read through the entire binder section for today, and there absolutely had not been any notation of an open bar. But if earlier was any indication, if Sydney said no, Hannah would call Tad, and Tad would say to do what she was told. Right?

"Fine," Sydney snapped back. "Open bar, you're sure? That could get expensive. Do you want just beer, or mixed drinks?"

Hannah waved a hand. "They can have whatever they want."

"Okay." Sydney shrugged and went though the kitchen to storage to pull out cases of alcohol. Rick and Elle were right behind her.

Rick scoffed. "Did I just hear what happened correctly? They didn't order alcohol, and now we're serving an open bar? Does this place always run like this? No offense."

Sydney wasn't offended. She shook her head. "I have no idea. I'm not usually running events alone. I know I'll get yelled at if she calls the owner, so if she wants an open bar, so be it. I'll probably get in trouble either way. At least someone will have some fun this way, and I'll have one person mad at me instead of a hundred. I don't suppose you know how to mix drinks?" she asked both of them.

Elle shook her head, but Rick nodded. "Sure, it's not that hard."

"Famous last words." Elle chuckled.

They all worked to stock the bar, and Rick jumped right in to serve. Once the bar was stocked, Sydney and Elle focused on beer and wine orders, leaving the mixed drinks to Rick. When that was under control, Sydney moved on to clearing dinner. Hours later, the attendees finally headed home, or to the hotel next door. Rick and Elle stayed and straightened tables, helped wash dishes, took out bags of trash, and helped make sure the place was all set for the next day.

They were wiping down the counters in the kitchen when Sydney pulled the binder back out and flipped to the next day. She calmly pushed it aside, put her arms on the counter, rested her head on her arms, and cried. The menu for the next day was worse, and Sydney was so far beyond exhausted, she just couldn't hold it together.

Elle tentatively put a hand on her back. "Sydney, you okay?" Sydney shook her head a little. She heard Elle pull a couple of stools over. Sydney gratefully sat on one but kept her head down and her eyes closed. Her head snapped up when Elle started cursing. "What kind of job is this?" she exclaimed, flipping through the binder. "You're expected to do all of this by yourself? How? Who did you piss off for this kind of torture?"

Rick pulled the book over, glanced at it, and pushed it back. "I have no idea what the problem is."

Sydney let Elle explain, as she was all fired up. "To prepare this menu? Will take careful prep and all night. This isn't reasonable for one person. There should be a whole team. The pastries for breakfast alone would take hours. Some of the salads are supposed to set overnight. Quit, Sydney. Let's just walk away right now. No job is worth this."

Sydney picked her head up, her lashes still wet with tears. "I can't," she whispered. "But you can go home. You've both been amazing today. Thank you so much. Please thank Ice for me. I don't even know how he knew I needed you, but I'm so grateful."

Elle shook her head. "No way. I'm not going anywhere. What kind of friend would I be if I left you to this," she gestured widely and seemed at a loss for words, finally settling on, "disaster! Right, Rick?"

He wasn't paying attention and said, "Ow," and nearly dropped his phone when she poked him.

"Here's what we're going to do," Elle said, clapping her hands and taking charge with just as much energy as she'd had when she arrived. "We're going to make coffee, and after a little nap, we're going to tackle this menu, and you're going to tell your new bestie—me, in case you were wondering—why we're doing this."

Sydney put her head back down. "A nap sounds lovely," she muttered, closing her eyes again. "Set a timer?" she asked no one in particular.

Sydney startled awake at the smell of blueberry

muffins, fresh out of the oven. She checked her watch and jumped off the stool, realizing she'd lost two hours. She had to blink several times to understand what she was seeing. Elle and Rick weren't the only ones navigating the kitchen and working through food prep. Ice and Ward were also wearing aprons and working.

"You woke her up!" Elle admonished.

Ward spun to face her, and Sydney threw her arms around his neck, sobbing. He wrapped his arms around her and held on tight. "What are you all doing here?" she choked out.

Ward rubbed her back gently, and Ice answered simply, "You needed help. Not that most of us have any idea what we're doing, but we're figuring it out."

"But how?" she asked, still confused and expecting this to all be a dream. If this was a dream, she didn't want to wake up. Ward's embrace felt too good.

Ward's voice rumbled under her ear. "We may have been stalking the event center's website to see what was going on. Ice snuck in at lunch and checked out the situation. It was dire, so he called in reinforcements. We would've been here earlier, but I didn't think my presence at this particular conference would've been wise."

"Thank you. All of you."

Ward didn't want to let Sydney go. She felt right in his arms. It was a shame she'd woken up. When he and Ice had arrived, Elle was working methodically through the recipes for the morning's array of muffins, breads, and cinnamon rolls. Rick was keeping an eye on things and retrieving ingredients for her.

Sydney had looked uncomfortable, perched on a stool with her head on her arms, but she'd been sound asleep. They'd tried to be quiet, but they must've forgotten the longer they were there. Rick had texted Ice the gist of the situation, but Ward hadn't believed it until he'd seen it for himself: the impossible menu and schedule for the next day, with only Sydney's name on the staff list, and Sydney so exhausted she could sleep through this chaos.

He hated this for her. He was happy to be here, to help in even a small way. But he wanted her out of this situation. He wanted to take Tad down a peg. Scratch that. He wanted to ground Tad into the dirt under his heel and make him suffer. And he wanted Belinda to be right there with him. Ward wasn't sure how involved she was in Tad's businesses, but she was Sydney's stepmom. She was a mom. She should be nurturing. She should be protecting Sydney from this abuse, and instead she was at least letting it happen, if not actively participating in it. It was despicable.

It wasn't lost on Ward that he was holding Belinda to a standard his own mom hadn't even met, but he'd seen how much Sydney cared for her sister. Her love for Ava was a boundless, selfless love he hadn't known was possible, and he wanted Sydney to have that kind of love in return. She deserved it more than anyone he knew. He wasn't sure he could be that for her, but she made him want to try.

Ice and Elle were bantering about something, but Ward wasn't paying attention. Sydney looked up at him, and he was lost. She pulled back a little and thanked him again.

"I wish you'd called me," he whispered.

"I couldn't," she confided.

"Why not?"

She looked around the kitchen and returned her eyes to his. "The only phone is that one. Tad knows everything that happens in this place, and he monitors the phone. I hope he's not paying attention to what's going on here, but it'll be worth it if he gets mad. I needed the nap, and I really, really appreciate everyone being here, losing sleep, and working so hard, even though I can't be a friend back."

Everyone else shrugged off her thanks and continued what they'd been doing. Ward ran his hands down her arms and interlaced her fingers with his. "Tad isn't going to know unless he shows up here personally. Ice hacked the cameras. Tad might wonder why you aren't home when it looks like no one is here, but he doesn't know about us." He meant the collective "us" including Ice, Elle, and Rick, but he liked the idea of just being an "us" with Sydney.

She looked confused but shrugged. "I'd rather have him upset that I didn't come home than have a hundred angry attendees in the morning. I don't think he'll show up here. But really, Ice, you're a hacker?"

He laughed. "Just a security guy. I know systems like this. Not a big deal."

She shook her head. "Whatever. Where are we? What can I do?" She yawned and rubbed her eyes.

Elle covered up the binder on the counter. "Nothing at all. We've got this. Ward, go find my new friend somewhere to crash."

"Yes, ma'am." He grinned.

Sydney resisted, but Elle stopped her. "You still need to serve all of those people again in the morning. You need some rest. Go."

Ward took her hand again and led her out of the kitchen. "Surely there's furniture more comfortable somewhere in this building than the kitchen stools and stacking chairs?" He found it curious that she just shrugged. They walked down the hallway and found the office, but Sydney wouldn't go in. There was only a desk chair in there, anyway. "Tad's space?" he asked her.

"Kind of. He isn't here much. He's been spending most of his time at Black lately, but it still feels like his space." Ward didn't miss her shudder. He squeezed her hand and continued down the hall. At the end, stairs led down a floor. At the bottom of the stairs, another few smaller meeting rooms were open, each with different sized tables and chairs. Unlike the spaces upstairs, these hadn't been updated in decades. Ward was about to give up hope when they opened the final door.

"Bingo!" The last room was a large game room with several groupings of furniture, including large sofas and recliners, along with a pool table, TVs, and gaming consoles. This would be a great place to bring a group to kick back and relax. He wondered why this room wasn't publicized on the website. He and Ice had been all over the websites for all of Tad's establishments. He pulled Sydney gently over to one of the couches and found a blanket on the back of one of the chairs. She sat on the edge, as if she was going to stand right up again.

He brought the blanket over and stood in front of her, studying her wild hair and the darkness under her eyes. She took his hand and just held on. "Will you stay with me?" she whispered. Ward's heart constricted. He nodded and sat beside her, pulling her down to lay on the couch. She fit nicely, tucked against him, and he covered them both with the blanket.

"I don't know how to let everyone else take over and

do my stuff for me," she confided. "I've never had that. You're lucky to have people to count on."

Ward held her just a little closer, tucking her hair out of his face. Tension slowly released as she relaxed in his arms. "They're your friends now too, Syd. When you need something, just ask. They'll be there."

Sydney managed to drift off to sleep, but Ward couldn't turn off her words, on repeat, running through his brain. *"You're lucky to have people to count on."* He was privileged. He'd never for a day gone without. He had a roof over his head (a very nice one), plenty of food in the fridge, complete autonomy over how he spent every day, and family and friends. He was light on the friends front, but Ice was solid, and he'd never felt like he needed more close friends. He had his choice of women to spend time with.

He had it all. And he never really appreciated it. He appreciated Ice's friendship, but he'd looked down on his father for his relationships. He'd kept women and other potential friends at arm's length until Sydney unintentionally drew his attention to his own excess.

He'd slept mere minutes when Ice woke him with a nudge to his shoulder. He nodded to let Ice know he was awake and took just another minute to enjoy Sydney's peaceful sleep. He whispered, "Syd, good morning."

She startled and nearly fell off the couch, but he chuckled and pulled her back. She relaxed in his arms again but cleared her throat. "Thank you. I slept so well. I don't want to go back up there and face the day." She snuggled back into him.

"Same. What would you be doing today if you were in control of your day? If you didn't have a bunch of obnoxious businesspeople expecting you to wait on them?"

She was silent for so long, he wondered if she'd fallen back to sleep. He wouldn't have blamed her. Finally, she answered, "I don't even know. I wouldn't mind starting the day like this. Maybe a leisurely breakfast. Nothing fancy. But for the rest of the day? I don't know. There are a lot of things I'd like to do. Maybe go to the zoo. Find a place to get gelato. Go on a hike." She shrugged. "Simple things."

"This morning, before we go, maybe you can write a letter to Ava. We can make copies and mail it to her at all of the schools. We'll put my phone number and a PO Box on it, so she can reach out. We'll find her and get you free of all of this."

Sydney stretched and pushed up to sit. Her hair was pointing all directions, and Ward thought she was more beautiful than any of the women he'd been photographed with. He sat up when she stood and chuckled as she tried to tame her hair.

"I'm sure I look ridiculous. It isn't fair," she said, gesturing vaguely at Ward. "You look the same. Are you even real?"

He stood and ran his fingers through her hair. "You're beautiful, Syd." He enjoyed the blush that rushed to her cheeks. "Let's get this day started."

They headed back up the stairs and stopped at the restrooms in the hallway. Ward stared at himself in the mirror for a minute, trying to figure out what she meant. His hair was sticking up oddly too, but he kept it pretty short. He thought he looked rumpled. When he got back to the kitchen, coffee was waiting for him, and Ice had his keys in hand.

"We're going to figure out the phone situation today, right?" Ward asked him. It bothered him that Sydney didn't have a way to reach out. Ice nodded. Sydney joined them, looking put together once more.

Elle filled her in on all of the prep work that had been done. It was still early, barely four, but they all needed to get home and catch a few hours of sleep themselves. Sydney hugged Elle tightly, and Elle hung on. When she let go and moved on to Ice, Ward grabbed Elle and hugged her himself. It might have been the first time ever, but he couldn't find words to tell her how much he appreciated her support, her open friendliness. She patted him on the back.

"I like her," she said quietly. "She's good for you. Don't break her heart."

"She might break mine," he admitted in a whisper. Elle shook her head and turned away, grabbing her husband's hand.

"Thanks for putting up with us barging in and taking over, Sydney. I hope I'll see you again soon," Rick said. He and Elle grabbed their things and left. Ice put on his jacket and waited for Ward in the doorway.

"Wait, the letter," Sydney reminded him. She rushed over to the office and came back with paper. She sat on one of the stools and stared at the blank page for a minute.

Ice came back over and stood beside Ward. "What letter?" he asked.

"For us to copy and mail to Ava at all of the boarding schools we found."

"Makes sense. I've tried reaching out to a few schools, but their privacy policies are pretty strict," Ice said.

Sydney nodded. "I didn't have any luck as her sister either, and I was afraid someone would alert Belinda." She finished writing and handed it over. "You'll add contact information?"

They both assured her they would. Ice folded the letter and put it in his bag with his laptop. "The cameras are going to revert to the live feed in a few minutes, Ward, we need to get out of here."

He nodded and forced himself to put his jacket on. "You'll be okay?" he asked, knowing full well she would nod.

"I'll be great," she assured him, forcing a smile. "I got the best sleep I've had in a long time, and so much is done for me that it'll be a relatively easy day. I can't thank you both enough. Take a muffin with you. And drive carefully, okay?"

Ward's stomach rumbled, and he accepted the giant muffin she handed him. He couldn't bring himself to say goodbye and just awkwardly waved instead, following Ice out a side door.

Once they were in the car, Ice asked, "Did you sleep?"

"A little, not much. A power nap will work. I'll be at the office on time. You need some sleep, though."

Ice nodded. "I'll catch a few hours, and then I'll take care of the phone. I'll ask Elle to send the letters out. Hopefully we can get them out today."

Ward thanked him as they arrived at home. They parted ways in the elevator, and Ward collapsed into bed. He slept hard for a couple of hours and woke disoriented. He'd woken from a vivid dream where he frantically searched for a little blonde girl who kept disappearing around corners, just out of reach. He was certain she was his daughter, and she was in danger. His heart was racing, and it took a minute to clear his head and fully wake. It had felt so real. The idea of having kids had never crossed his mind, even for a moment.

He went about his day as normally as possible. It took effort to greet Chantelle without thinking about Sydney and how differently they were treated in the same household. Chantelle looked like she had everything she needed. She seemed well rested and well dressed, and she had been ordering in pricey lunches each day. She had a cushy office job.

He knew he wasn't the easiest person to work for, but he'd never once forced or even asked an employee to work an all-nighter. He focused on treating Chantelle exactly the same as he had before he knew about her family, and it must've worked because she was just as bubbly as ever. She followed him into his office, and he stopped her.

"Sorry, Chantelle, there's something I need to work on first thing this morning. Can we meet later instead?"

She pouted, paused for a moment as if hoping he'd change his mind, and nodded, going back to her desk. She left him alone for the rest of the morning, and Ward buried himself in work.

It had been a good day. Sydney smiled to herself as the last attendee walked out the door, Hannah right behind them. Somehow, the whole day passed without a hitch. The prep work that everyone had done while she slept helped her keep on top of the agenda for the day, and she was thankful every time she reached for something and it was ready to go. The attendees enjoyed the food, and there wasn't another call for alcohol, so no one got drunk and handsy, and she didn't have to figure out how to mix drinks.

Sydney made her way through the space, resetting tables and chairs for the next event and cleaning up. She was tired after a long day of work, but she wasn't anywhere near as exhausted as she had been. She didn't remember ever sleeping as well as she had in Ward's arms. He'd been warm and solid, and she'd felt safe with him. She couldn't have slept down there if he hadn't stayed. She would've spent the night on edge, wondering if someone was going to come in and worrying about the day ahead. How Tad thought anyone could handle that project singlehandedly was beyond her, but maybe that was the point. He wanted her to fail spectacularly. She couldn't understand why when it would only tarnish Keller's reputation.

By the time everything was cleaned up, it was late and dark, but she didn't mind. The cold air felt good against her face. She couldn't stop smiling, even when she missed the bus and had to wait. When an older man arrived at the bus stop in a ragged coat and torn pants, she nodded to him and stepped away. He kept slowly moving closer, and Sydney cringed, but she had to hold her ground to stay at the bus stop.

"Pretty girl," he muttered.

"Thank you," she answered politely.

He didn't say anything else, and he thankfully stopped inching closer. When the bus arrived, he didn't get on, and Sydney wondered if he'd be okay. It was still near freezing outside, and she didn't like the idea that he might not have a place to go. It was too bad that Keller sat empty and warm all night when there were people that needed somewhere to get out of the cold.

When she got off the bus, she paused before heading home. She didn't want to, but she put one foot in front of the other. Anything could await her. Everyone could be asleep. That would be the best-case scenario. But she hadn't forgotten how upset they'd been the last time she hadn't come home.

The lights were on. All of them. She took a deep

breath and forced herself to take the steps calmly. The door opened before she reached it. Maybe they'd tell her she couldn't come home. At least then, she could find a way to call Ward. He wouldn't let her sleep outside and freeze.

Tad held on to his anger until she was fully in the house. He closed and locked the door and then whirled on her. She fought her instinct to shrink away and stood her ground.

"Where have you been? You were warned the last time you were gone overnight not to let it happen again," he roared.

Sydney should've been prepared with what to say. She knew he'd ask. But if she explained what actually happened, it wouldn't go over well. He'd tell her not to complain, even if she wasn't actually complaining. She tried anyway. "There was too much prep work to do for today. I stayed at work to get it done. I think the event went well." She hoped focusing on the happy client would distract him from his anger, but his face was getting redder, not calmer.

"Liar! I checked the cameras. You weren't working all night. I don't know what funny business happened, but it will not happen again."

Right. She'd momentarily forgotten that Ice manipulated the camera feed. She just nodded. What else could she say or do? Tad grabbed her shoulder and shoved her through the house to the basement stairs. She very nearly fell down, barely managing to grab onto the handrail and right herself as he slammed the door closed and locked it, leaving her in complete darkness.

She closed her eyes and shuddered. It was cold down here, and she struggled to recall what it looked like in the light, what she would run into. She carefully stepped down, one step at a time.

At the bottom, she paused and looked around, hoping that her eyes would adjust just enough to be able to make out shapes. There weren't any windows, so there wasn't even a sliver of moonlight to help guide her. She sat on the bottom step and huddled into her jacket and Ward's hoodie that she still wore beneath it. It still smelled a little like him, a fresh mix of mint and lemon. If only she'd asked him to wear it again overnight ... but that would have sounded silly.

It was going to be a miserable night, but she couldn't regret it. She wouldn't. Not when she'd gained new friends. Friends that helped each other and laughed together. The teasing between Ice and his sister warmed Sydney's heart. She missed her sister fiercely. It had been so many years since she'd actually seen and talked to her. She was afraid she wouldn't even recognize her. For the moment, Sydney clung to the thought that Ava was safely at school, and Sydney's new friends were going to find her.

Sydney couldn't get comfortable. She spent all night drifting off and jolting awake. In the morning, she heard the sounds of the household waking and starting their day, and she made her way back up the dark stairs and knocked. No one answered.

When she heard voices in the kitchen, she tried again, and still she was ignored. The thought that she was stuck down here indefinitely started to trigger panic. She needed a bathroom, and she would need to eat something at some point. She'd never given a thought to the light switch being at the top of the stairs outside the door, but now she realized just how bad her situation was.

Don't panic, she reminded herself. She could figure this out. She could find a way out. Or she could figure out how to survive down here until Tad was done with his sadistic torture. She just needed a little bit of light. Whoever built this basement without even one, little window was evil, she decided. She heard everyone leave for work and almost cried, but she held herself together. This wasn't the end of the world. She apparently had a day off from work. She could work with this.

She made her way back down the stairs and reached out, feeling around. Her hand first found cobwebs, and she nearly shrieked. She took a deep breath and shook her hand off. Cobwebs didn't mean spiders, necessarily. The prickles she felt on her neck were her imagination playing tricks on her. Really.

She inched forward, shuffling her feet and feeling along the wall. It was painstaking, trying to pause and identify the things she ran across. She knew there should be extra food down here and hoped to find crackers or cereal or something, even if they were long forgotten and stale. She remembered Belinda going through a prepper stage and stashing essentials in case of an earthquake. It never made sense to Sydney. If there was an earthquake and the supplies were in the basement, the supplies would be under tons of rubble when they were needed. Locked downstairs in the dark, she didn't think it was silly anymore.

She eventually found the five-gallon buckets that contained first aid supplies, and she nearly cried. She was sure there would be a flashlight in there, and the bucket would be usable for her toilet needs for now. She hoped Tad would come to his senses and put her back to work soon, but her bladder couldn't wait much longer.

She pulled the lid off the first bucket she found and went through each item before setting it aside. The flashlight was near the top, and it didn't turn on. Sydney's heart dropped, and she worked to calm her breathing. Hyperventilating wouldn't help.

Batteries. There must be batteries. She continued going through item after item. At the very bottom of the bucket, she finally felt a battery-shaped package. She prayed that they would still work. They had been there for years.

Sydney carefully opened the package and found the place to put the batteries in the flashlight. After a few misstarts, she finally got them in the right direction. The flashlight took a good shake to get started, but suddenly the room was flooded with light.

Sydney had to cover her eyes to help them adjust. She sighed in relief, but it was short lived as she looked around the basement. It was a filthy mess. It was a miracle she'd gotten over to the emergency bucket unscathed with most of the floor covered in boxes, furniture, tools, and other junk. She hoped she'd be released today, because she didn't want to try to sleep down here again. There wasn't a good flat space to lay down, and there was nothing even remotely clean to lay on.

She gathered the supplies from the bucket and found space on a shelf for them, used the bucket, and set the lid back on. She'd lost her appetite for now, but she'd keep the emergency rations handy for later. She made her way back to the stairs and sat, turning off the flashlight to conserve the battery.

She settled in to wait and entertained herself thinking about what she wanted from her life once Ava was free. Ward's question about what she would do with her day if she was free opened up the floodgates. She didn't know. As long as she could see Ava and support herself, and maybe spend time with her new friends, she didn't care where she lived or what kind of work she did.

Ward hadn't seen Sydney in over a week, and he worried more with every day that passed. There had been events at Keller, but she hadn't staffed them. They hadn't seen her walking between the diner and Black. He was at a loss. He wanted to see her, to know she was okay. He wanted to tell her that Elle had mailed out the letters. All they could do now was wait. He jumped every time his phone rang, hoping it was Ava. Ice was checking the new mailbox they had opened every day.

Ward was adjusting his cufflinks when Ice walked in and sat heavily at Ward's kitchen counter. Another Friday night, another black-tie event. Ward used to enjoy playing with the media, even if he didn't enjoy the events themselves, but today he wanted nothing more than to stay home. It looked like Ice felt the same.

"Everything okay?"

Ice scowled at him and gestured to Ward's tux. "We're really doing this? This event is nothing more than

Jameson Harris showing off his success. What are you hoping to accomplish by going?"

He tugged at his sleeves. "What do I ever hope to accomplish at these? Put in an appearance, remind people that I exist and am part of their circle, though I'm not sure why I care right now."

"Well that's something, I guess. Who is the arm candy tonight?"

Ward shrugged. "Going solo. You're my date. Congrats."

Ice stood and adjusted his tie. "Whatever. Ready?"

Ward nodded, and they headed down to the car. This year's pinnacle event was being held at an exclusive restaurant at the top of the tallest building in the city. Ward could appreciate the view, but he didn't care about a single person in attendance. None of them were his friends, aside from Ice. He would rub elbows, chat vaguely about projects and possibilities, line up meetings, and hopefully come away with something worthwhile. This was work just as much as the time he spent at his desk every day.

An hour into the event, there was commotion at the entrance, and Tate burst into the room. He scanned the guests and zeroed in on Ward. He charged over, red faced. Ice stepped between them just as Tate reached Ward, pointing a furious finger at him. He shoved against Ice to no avail.

"You!" Tate shouted. "I can't believe you! Beware!" he yelled, gesturing to the rest of the attendees. "Ward

McKinney is not to be trusted! He'll sweep projects right out from underneath you!"

The audience tittered, but Ward rocked back on his heels and tilted his head, considering Tate's outburst. Ice continued to keep him more than an arm's length away. Tate continued to bluster, repeating himself. "Have you nothing to say for yourself?" he demanded.

Ward just shrugged. "It's business, Robert. Nothing more, nothing less. We just had a conversation. No NDA, no details. I didn't steal your project, I just enhanced my own. Yours could still be successful."

Tate again tried to push past Ice, swearing a blue streak. The guest of honor's security detail assisted Ice with removing him from the event, and Jameson approached Ward and shook his hand. "Sorry, he wasn't on the guest list. He shouldn't have been allowed in."

Ward shook his head. "I apologize for the drama. I knew taking on a similar project in his backyard was going to push his buttons, and I can't apologize for that, but I didn't intend to bring disruption to your event."

Jameson grinned. "He's a fool. He's been trying to set up a meeting with me for weeks. Tell me more about this project?"

Ward filled him in on the conversation he'd had with Tate and the project he had well underway practically next door. "There's actually a building in between that you might be interested in," he offered. Jameson's portfolio was mostly real estate holdings, a mix of residential and commercial. "It's a bit run down now, and the current owners want a fortune for it, but perhaps they'd entertain an offer from you."

"I'll look into it. It was good to see you, Ward. Enjoy the rest of your evening." Jameson clapped a hand to his shoulder and moved on to greet another guest.

Ice returned with a drink in his hand, which he handed to Ward. "That was the most excitement I've seen at one of these in a while. Good to know I'm here for a reason, I guess."

Ward looked his friend over. "I think our work here is done. Unless you think Robert is waiting just outside to ambush me again. Maybe we should stay a bit longer?"

Ice shook his head. "Doubtful, but one of Jameson's guys will keep an eye out when we leave, just in case. Tate's more determined than I expected."

They made their way back through the crowd, and a few people stopped Ward to chat about Tate. There was clearly a reason he wasn't invited. No one in the room respected him. They couldn't believe that he had the nerve to accuse Ward of stealing a project when he hadn't even protected his own ideas. Ward was encouraged by the response, and he was glad he'd attended. This was his community.

They made the drive home quickly, but Ward was lost in thought and didn't get out of the car right away.

"Still nothing from Ava?" Ice asked.

Ward shook his head. "Nothing from Sydney, either. She has to turn up sooner or later, right? I'm worried about her."

"I can start asking around, go to the diner and Black,

if you want." They got out of the car and stepped into the elevator.

"Not Black. Tad spends too much time there, from what I've gathered, and I don't want him to know I have any interest in Sydney—or in Black."

Ice's gaze whipped over to Ward. "You're interested in Black?"

Ward shrugged. "I'm interested in making Tad and Belinda suffer. I don't have a plan yet, but I will."

"Anything you need from me?"

Ward thought about it. "Just keep an eye out for her."

Ice went home, and Ward spent the rest of the evening researching and plotting ways to make Tad's life difficult. He thought back to the night he'd met Sydney. She'd been running scared, terrified, and the direction she'd been running from could've easily been Black. She'd been in her standard uniform, the black button-down shirt and black pants that she wore to all of the businesses. He doubted she'd been running from Tad. Ward had seen the man. He was nearly as wide as he was tall and looked like walking across a room would be a workout. Sydney could outrun him. He must have sent someone after her.

Belinda was a different nut to crack. It would be easy enough to fire her. He could find a reason that would pass legal. He was furious that she'd used her position to put her daughter at his assistant's desk. He was glad it seemed Sydney was right and Chantelle wasn't the brightest crayon in the box. He didn't think she was doing any snooping or retaining any information to feed back to

Belinda, but he wondered what her angle was. Why did she want her daughter at his side? Was it just a match-making ploy, or was she hoping for some information to use against him?

He decided to let a bit of information about a project loose around Chantelle. Misinformation. And see where it went from there. If he did it right and Belinda took the bait, it could be publicly embarrassing for her, which would be delightful. He smiled and put things into motion.

SIXTEEN

SYDNEY

Sydney had no way of knowing how long she'd been in the dark. With no daylight, she never knew if it was morning or night. She'd lost track of how many times she'd heard activity in the kitchen, her hopes raised that she would finally be released. In between those fleeting moments of hope, desolation took over, leaving her feeling forgotten and alone. Her whole body ached. She was out of water, and the food hadn't lasted long. Most of the packets in the emergency kit hadn't been edible or required heating.

The sound of the door lock mechanism didn't register at first. There had been sounds before that meant nothing. She didn't bother trying to get up. When a bright shard of light shone down the stairs, Sydney covered her eyes and shrank away.

"Oh, gross, Sydney, clean up that disgusting stench!" Belinda's voice carried down the stairs. "You are to be at Black in an hour." She whirled away.

Sydney wondered at first if she had hallucinated. She slowly opened her eyes, the light still burning them. She scrambled up the stairs on unsteady limbs and wobbled to the bathroom, tossing herself in the shower. The water wasn't hot enough to burn off the layers of dust and fear that clung to her. She scrubbed and scrubbed but still felt filthy. She dried and dressed and just wanted to collapse into bed, but getting out of the house was also appealing. If she wasn't here, they couldn't lock her in the basement again.

She grabbed a bottle of water and a granola bar from the kitchen and rushed outside. She hadn't looked at her watch when Belinda told her she had an hour, so she had no idea if she was running late, but she spent longer in the shower than usual. She found that she couldn't rush. Her body adamantly refused to move any faster than a slow, unsteady walk. Sheer willpower pushed her forward and got her through the doors of Black. She collapsed onto the bench in the locker room and took several long minutes to convince her body to start moving again.

"Where the hell is the dishwasher?" someone bellowed from the kitchen.

Sydney took a deep breath and stood. She forced herself out to the kitchen to start work. The chef and bussers were grumbling about her absence, but she ignored them and did her best to get the job done. She was successful for a couple of hours, but every minute was harder than the one before. Her body was shaking. Her mind was foggy.

When a plate shattered at her feet, she stood there, staring at it. The thought of going down to the cellar to retrieve more plates barely entered her mind before she shut it down. She couldn't. She couldn't go down into the dark. She couldn't risk being shut in again. Her chest tightened, and her heart raced. She was spiraling in panic but couldn't stop.

A manager grabbed her and started yelling at her to clean it up, but Sydney just stood there, dazed. The manager threw her hands up in the air. "Go home! And don't come to work wasted again!"

Sydney shook her head. She wasn't wasted. She was exhausted. But who was she to argue? She wasn't in any condition to work. She walked out through the employee exit and started walking aimlessly down the sidewalk. Tad was going to know she hadn't finished her shift, but she didn't want to go home. She walked without really paying attention to where she was going. Eventually, she found herself at the diner and pushed through the door.

Leah was standing at the hostess stand, chatting with the evening hostess. A friendly face was a welcome sight. "Sydney? Is that you?" she asked. Leah approached and wrapped an arm around her. "Come sit down, dear. Where have you been?"

"Sorry," she whispered, unsure what to say. Leah guided her to a booth in the back, and Sydney dropped onto the seat.

Leah placed a mug of hot chocolate in front of her in no time. She sat across from Sydney, quiet for a minute. "Are you okay?"

Sydney lifted a shoulder. "I haven't been feeling well. I'm probably on the schedule in the morning. I should go home." She started to stand, but Leah stopped her, reaching out to place her hand on Sydney's arm.

"Get some rest for a while. I can give you a ride home when I get off in two hours, if you'd like. You shouldn't be alone like this. You can rest here for a little while, okay?"

Sydney nodded and settled back down. She wrapped her hands around the warm mug and watched steam rise. The sweet drink was too rich, so she took very small sips, but it warmed her insides. She finished it and put her head down on her arms on the table. Staying here might not be the smartest move, but Tad didn't come here, and she didn't think he kept a very close eye on the place. She'd just do as Leah said and rest for a little while.

"Sydney?" Leah nudged her some time later. "I'm about to head home. Would you like that ride?"

Sydney woke groggy but feeling a bit better than she had earlier. She blinked. She realized Leah had asked her something. "Sorry, what did you ask?"

Leah looked at her with compassion in her eyes. "I asked if you would like a ride home, but I'd rather know if you'll be safe there first?"

Sydney flinched and moved to stand. She couldn't have anyone knowing what was going on at home. She couldn't risk it. Not until Ava was safe. "I'll be fine. Thank you, Leah, for being so kind."

Leah watched her for a long moment before getting up again herself. "If you're sure. Take care of yourself,

Sydney. You can't take care of others in your life if you don't take care of yourself first."

Sydney nodded. It was good advice, but it wasn't practical for her while her life was outside of her own control. She could accept Leah's kindness, though. "A ride would be great, if you're sure you don't mind. Thank you."

They walked out to Leah's older Corolla together. "Do you often work nights?" Sydney asked. "You're here a lot of mornings."

Once they were in and the heater was cranked to clear the windshield, Leah answered, "Not usually, but I've been picking up extra shifts where I can. My daughter was sick for a while. She's doing better, but the medical bills are insane."

"I'm glad she's doing better. She's lucky to have you." Sydney realized too late that she should've kept that to herself. It made her sound needy.

"Thank you," Leah replied, oblivious to Sydney's inner battle. When the windows were sufficiently defogged, Leah pulled out, and Sydney directed her to her home. She thought about being dropped off around the block, but she was still too tired to expend any more energy than she had to.

"Thank you, Leah. You're the best," Sydney said as she got out and closed the door. Leah waited at the curb until Sydney was inside. It was late, and the house was dark. She supposed they expected her to work late and weren't waiting up for her. She trudged up the stairs, doing her best to make her footsteps as quiet as possible, and collapsed into bed. She needed to do laundry. She missed Ward's sweater, but everything she'd been wearing smelled rancid. She needed to deal with the bucket downstairs, but she would do that in the daylight with the door propped open.

She fell into an exhausted sleep and only woke when her name was shrieked up the stairs. Belinda expected her breakfast. Sydney padded down the stairs, pulling her hair out of her face and into a ponytail. Once in the kitchen, she went through the motions of preparing breakfast and tuned out their chatter until Ward's name popped up. She'd forgotten that Chantelle got to spend her days in Ward's office. A stab of jealousy pierced her gut, and she struggled to keep her expression neutral.

Chantelle was bouncing in her seat. "It's going to be so great! He'll be able to unveil it at the anniversary party!"

Sydney had no idea what Chantelle was so excited about, but she was happy for Ward that he had something good going on. She desperately wished to see him again. Chantelle continued rambling, moving on to raving about the suit he'd been wearing and how rugged he looked when he didn't shave. She wondered aloud if he'd kiss her back if she kissed him. Sydney coughed to cover up her horrified reaction.

The thought of Chantelle on Ward's arm shouldn't make her feel so ill. Chantelle was exactly the type of woman he was always photographed with. But he deserved better. He deserved someone who actually cared about who he was and not just that he was attractive and rich.

Thankfully, Belinda and Chantelle left for work without paying any attention to Sydney. Tad hadn't come out for coffee this morning, and she wondered if that was a good thing or a bad thing. With any luck, he was ill and didn't notice that she'd left Black early.

Hoping he stayed away a little bit longer, Sydney opened the door to the basement. She shuddered at the smell and at the thought of going back down those stairs. She had to. She knew she had to. No one else was going to take care of it. She propped the door open as solidly as she could, rushed down the stairs, grabbed the bucket, and rushed back up. She closed the door and stood against it for a moment, overwhelmed with relief that she hadn't been trapped again. She took care of the bucket, threw her laundry in the washer, and got ready for work.

Without Tad's instructions, she assumed she should go to the diner and then to Black. It had been her most normal routine on non-event days, and it seemed like the safest assumption.

When she walked into the diner, she found it fully staffed. There was nothing for her to do. Leah was there, but she was busy, and Sydney just waved to her before stepping back out into the cold morning. She walked to Keller just to make sure there weren't any events, and the place was quiet. She didn't know what to do with herself. She walked to the park and sat on a bench, watching birds picking through garbage and runners going about their day.

What might have been minutes or hours later, someone sat beside her. She started to pull away but the cologne that wafted her way was the scent that had comforted her every day. She looked over and found the one person, other than Ava, that she most wanted to see. She blinked, struggling to hold back the tears that threatened to spill. It took effort to keep herself from throwing her arms around him.

Ward held out a hand, and she slipped hers in his without hesitation, absorbing his warmth.

"How did you know I was here?"

"We didn't. It had been so long since I'd seen you that I was worried. We had coffee at the diner this morning and asked our waitress if she'd seen you. She seemed nice. Hopefully we didn't cause any trouble by asking about you. She said you'd been in and left. We've been looking for you."

"Was it Leah? She is nice. Thanks for seeking me out." She squeezed his hand, hard. "I've missed you," she whispered, anguish coloring her words.

"Are you okay?" he asked, leaning closer and studying her face.

She couldn't lie to him, but she couldn't tell him the truth. "I've been better," she admitted. "But I'll survive. I have this long, right?"

Ward grumbled. A phone appeared between them, and Sydney startled. She shouldn't have been surprised that Ice was behind them, but she was. Ward took the phone and handed it to Sydney. "I hate that you don't have a phone. Please take this one and stash it somewhere. Our contact information is saved with our initials."

Sydney nodded and took it. Ice handed her a charger as well. She slipped them both in her pocket. "Thank you."

Ice bent down and shared quietly, "There's also one under the sink in the ladies' rooms at the diner, Black, and Keller. Elle will make sure they're charged periodically."

Sydney turned to stare at him. "Really? That's ... too much."

Both men shook their heads. "It's not enough. But it's something we can do for now. We haven't heard from Ava yet, but letters are starting to come back marked undeliverable or 'not at this address,' so we know they're making their way through the postal service. It's just a matter of time before one reaches her."

Sydney nodded, still overwhelmed by the effort they'd gone to. "I don't know how to thank you."

"Don't. It isn't necessary. Just focus on getting through each day and keeping Tad and Belinda happy until we find her. After that, there will be no reason for you to stay with them, right?"

She thought through what that would mean. If they knew where Ava was, she could talk to her. She could make sure Ava knew she was loved. "As long as her tuition is paid for through the end of the semester, she should be okay, unless Tad tries to pull her out anyway."

Ward nodded. "We'll make sure she's safe before you

walk away from them. Hang in there, Sydney." He leaned over and kissed her hair.

"Don't leave yet?" she whispered.

He sat with her for a few minutes, his shoulder against hers and his thumb brushing against her hand. The longer they stayed, the more aware she became that they were out in the open, where anyone could see them together. She pulled away and stood up. She wanted so badly to hug him, but she resisted and wrapped her arms around herself. She backed away and thanked them both before leaving. Every step away from them took effort.

She took the long way to Black and hesitated before going in. Maybe she was replaced here too. If Tad replaced her in the schedule and didn't put her back to work, he could have already pulled Ava and she wouldn't know. She prayed that wasn't the case, that Ava was still safe, and that he was just playing with her.

SEVENTEEN

WARD

Ward sat back in his chair, a small smile on his face. It had been a long few weeks, but this weekend's anniversary party was going to be a highlight of the year on so many levels. He'd decided to keep it a surprise from the guests of honor. They knew they were attending a black-tie event, but their assistant kept the purpose of the event vague. Ward was feeling good about celebrating their relationship and felt lighter than he had in years. Chantelle was still blissfully happy in her position, and Ward was content to let her think she was doing actual work.

"Excuse me, sir," Chantelle interrupted his musings with a tap to his doorframe. "There is someone here to see you."

He frowned at her. "Who?"

Robert Tate waltzed into his office, and Ward's scowl deepened.

Chantelle left them alone, and Ward hadn't seen

her face long enough to judge if she'd intentionally and knowingly left him with someone who had gone after him at a public event. It had been a desperate move, no matter how much Ward deserved it. Ward closed the door. He didn't need her overhearing anything.

"Robert," he greeted with a tight smile, gesturing to the guest chairs in front of his desk. He pulled out his phone and texted Ice, who responded immediately.

Tate is in my office.

On my way.

"What can I do for you today?" Not that he intended to do Tate any favors.

Robert's face reddened, and he shifted with indecision, but he finally eased down onto one of the chairs. Ward sank back into his own chair and waited.

"You took my project from me, and I hear you've been asking around about what else I'm working on. What did I ever do to you to make you my enemy?" The desperate plea turned Ward's stomach, but not with guilt. The man was weak, through and through.

"It's just business, Robert. You do the same. You see an opportunity, weigh it, and if it makes sense, you take it. I didn't take your project. You can still complete yours, it'll just have competition. What are you really doing here?"

Tate's eyes shifted around the office, to the door, and back to Ward. "I'm in trouble," he confided. Ward leaned forward in his chair and waited. "My investor backed out of the project. I need to replace him."

Ward shook his head. "I'm not investing in a competitor's property, and I've already declined." He paused, giving the illusion that he was thinking, but the chess pieces lined up nicely in his head. Finally, he said, "There may be something I find appealing in your portfolio, though, that could free up some cash for you."

Robert squinted and tilted his head. He swiped sweat from his brow. "What's that?"

Ward shrugged and leaned back. "I don't know yet, but if you wanted to put together a list of your holdings and their financials, I'd be happy to take a look and let you know." Robert pursed his lips. "It's the only way you might get some money from me," Ward reiterated.

Robert stood and wiped his hands on his slacks. "I'll put something together. I hope I'm not wasting my time."

Ward clapped him on the shoulder. "Tell you what. In good faith, you're invited to a black-tie event at Keller Event Center this weekend. I'll have Chantelle send you an invitation." He opened the door and ushered Robert out. Ice was standing near Chantelle's desk, watching them warily. Robert gave him a wide berth and offered them a half wave on his way to the elevator.

Ward looked to Chantelle, who nodded, asking, "Who was that? I'll send him an invitation."

Ice growled, "What do you mean, who was that? You let him into Ward's office and you didn't know who he was?" He leaned toward her with a look menacing enough that most people would be intimidated.

Chantelle ignored his ire, oblivious. "Security let him upstairs, I figured he was expected. Was that wrong?" She looked to Ward with wide, innocent eyes.

Ward gestured for Ice to back off. "Next time someone shows up without an appointment, get their name, and call Ice to confirm."

"Okay," she agreed cheerfully.

Ice followed him back into his office and closed the door. "What was that all about?"

A genuine smile spread across Ward's face. Things were coming together, and the buzz of impending victory hummed under his skin. "Good things, my friend. Better than I could've planned. Tate is desperately seeking money to finish his project."

Ice scowled. "You aren't going to give it to him."

"Not directly for that, no, of course not. But he has something I want. I haven't told him what yet. I'm going to let him sweat it out and put together a menu of sorts for me instead."

"Are you going to fill me in, or do I have to wait for the grand reveal?" Ice grumbled, sitting in the chair Robert had just vacated and tapping his fingers against the desk.

Ward pulled up a document on his computer and turned his monitor so that Ice could see. He may have just asked Tate to put together a list of his holdings, but Ward had already done his research.

Ice whistled and grinned. "This could be fun," he commented in a low voice. "No wonder you're so happy all of a sudden."

Ward stood and walked over to the windows overlooking the city. McKinney Enterprises owned a number of businesses throughout the area, but it was best known for facilitating mergers and flipping companies. They didn't often hold on to things. He wasn't sure what he wanted to do with Tate's holdings, but he could see possibilities.

It was just as appealing to keep them, grow them, and show Tate he was cursed as it would be to shut them down and erase him from the planet. It wasn't fair, he supposed, as Tate hadn't done anything except be average and make questionable partnership choices. Acknowledging that it wasn't fair wasn't changing Ward's trajectory.

"What's the plan for the rest of the day?" Ice asked, standing to join him.

"Board meeting in the morning. I'm not going to mention any of this yet, but I do need to prepare for it. Anniversary party this weekend. Chantelle has it pretty well planned, but there are a few things I need to go over with Tad at Keller, as much as that makes my skin crawl." He checked his watch. "Actually, I need to head over there now."

Ice nodded. Ward shut down his computer, and they walked out together.

Chantelle greeted them, still smiling. "Are you leaving for your meeting at the Keller Event Center? I'll let them know you're on your way."

"Thank you. Have a good evening," Ward replied without missing a step.

"That might be the nicest I've seen you treat her," Ice offered after the elevator doors closed.

Ward shrugged. "Now that I don't expect her to do any real work, I don't have any reason to be frustrated with her. Set the bar low, and you won't be disappointed, right?"

"I guess that's a strategy."

They walked to Keller from the McKinney building. Pots of purple and white crocuses decorated the entry, hopeful that spring was right around the corner. When they walked in, the place smelled overwhelmingly of roses, and Ward sneezed three times in rapid succession.

Tad appeared with a big smile on his face and his hand outstretched. "Welcome, gentlemen. Can I get you anything to drink?"

Ward was still sneezing and declined to shake hands. "Please tell me it will no longer smell like a floral shop died in here by Saturday?" he choked out.

Tad stepped back and frowned. He looked around, leading them into the main ballroom. Dozens and dozens of vases of red and white roses covered every surface throughout the room and much of the floor. "Sorry about this. There was a proposal here last night, and it appears that our staff have not yet disposed of the flowers. Everything will be perfect for your event, I assure you."

Ward fought to hide his cringe from Tad. He knew exactly who was going to have to deal with all of this and who was going to suffer Tad's wrath if things weren't perfect. He'd make it up to her. Tad led them through to the kitchen, where he opened the event binder on the counter. He consulted a page and opened the fridge, pulling out trays of food. Ice hung back in the doorway.

"Here are samples of the appetizers and desserts you've selected. I can heat up the main course samples, if you'd like."

Ward waved him away. "I've been to events here before. I'm not concerned about the quality of the food." Tad beamed with pride. Ward wanted to wipe the grin from his face but held it together. "Were there questions that you needed me here to answer, or are we wasting my time?"

Tad cleared his throat. "We just need to verify the details are set correctly and that you approve, and we'll be all set." He walked through the items in the binder, from start and end times, to alcohol orders, the menu, the seating configuration and music, and any other needs. It seemed accurate and complete to Ward. Chantelle had chosen well enough.

"These arrangements seem sufficient," Ward said, moving to leave.

"If I could ask a favor," Tad asked, prompting Ward to pause his retreat. "I understand this event is to honor your father. It would mean a great deal to my wife and I if we could attend. We've always had the utmost respect for him and what he's done for our community. Obviously, we wouldn't count ourselves in your billed headcount."

Ward gritted his teeth at the nerve of this man. He should be attending the event as an employee of the event center, as the person in charge, not as an attendee. But if he was focused on acting like a guest, maybe he'd cut Sydney some slack. Even the slightest possibility that agreeing would help her in some way had him giving in. "Fine," he ground out and picked up the pace. He brushed past Ice, through the sneeze-inducing floral room, and out into the fresh air.

"Did he really just have the nerve to ask for an invite to an event you're paying him to provide space and arrangements for?" Ice grumbled in exasperation when they were clear of the building. Ward just nodded. What more was there to say? "Unreal. And you went along with it."

"Now I have both Tad and Tate attending. I don't know what to do with that, but clearly something is wrong with me."

Ice chuckled. "At least he's not going to charge you for his place setting." He rolled his eyes.

Ward wasn't ready to go back to the office, or to go home. He walked toward the park instead.

Ice sobered. "She's not going to be there."

Ward puffed out a sigh. "I know. I just need some air. Especially after the rose attack. Don't ever let me do anything that stupid, and I'll do the same for you. Deal?"

Ice laughed and agreed. "Something as stupid as filling a room with roses, or proposing?"

Ward was quiet for a minute, and Ice stopped walking. "The roses," Ward muttered, focusing on the still water and the birds flying overhead. Ice opened his mouth to say something, but no words came out.

Ward knew what he was thinking. Very recently, he'd

been adamant that he'd never get close enough to someone to even consider tying himself to them. He wouldn't even sleep with the women who threw themselves at him. One of his biggest fears was to be manipulated and trapped with a pregnancy scare. His parents hadn't been happy together in the years before his mom left. Bringing a kid into a miserable relationship would be irresponsible. He wouldn't admit it, but he was starting to think that Ice had been right and he'd just been surrounding himself with the wrong women. He raised a hand. "Don't even say it. I know. Moving on. Do you think that taking advantage of Tate is a stupid, emotional move?"

Ice shrugged. "You're the business genius. I haven't seen the numbers. I'm sure your dad would weigh in if you need a second opinion."

Ward nodded. It was the obvious answer, but he'd needed to hear it. He respected his dad's experience and business acumen. As much as he wanted to take over the company and felt he was ready, he was glad to still have the old man at the helm for now. "I'll talk to him tomorrow. I don't suppose you're bringing a date to the party?"

Ice's head snapped around to face him. "Why would I do that?"

"It's a family event. You're family. And I don't think I'll need your official services for the evening. I don't expect Tate or anyone else to come at me again so soon, and I won't be inviting paparazzi attention."

Ice frowned. "You're going to another event solo?

People are going to start speculating about what's going on with you."

"Don't change the subject. We were talking about you bringing a date, not me." Ice's ears reddened, but he didn't say anything. Ward didn't miss a beat. "So there is someone. Who is she?" he asked, smiling.

"There isn't."

"There is, but you don't want to tell me?"

Ice rolled his eyes. "If you haven't noticed, I work a lot. I'm with you a lot. When am I supposed to date?"

Ward considered that, shoving his hands in his pockets and starting back the way they came. "Ask her to the party, Ice. You deserve better than a life keeping me out of trouble."

Ice shoved his shoulder. "I will, but cut it out. This sappy drama isn't you. If I minded, I'd say something. Or quit. Don't worry about me. You have enough on your plate." He wasn't wrong, but Ward wanted his friend to have a full, satisfying life.

If Sydney never saw another rose as long as she lived, it would still be too soon. Dozens of florists throughout the city delivered them all, filling the space with a shocking abundance of the red and white flowers. She could just imagine the surprise and delight the bride-to-be must have felt, seeing the lengths her new fiancé had gone to. Sydney hoped a photographer had been on hand to document the proposal.

Now, though, in the aftermath, Sydney was tasked with disposing of all of the flowers and cleaning up more petals than she could count. Her fingers stung from pinpricks of thousands of thorns, and her sense of smell may never return to normal. She could use a magician on hand, because she still needed to make a hundred vases disappear.

She was washing the last of the vases, which were now scattered all over every flat surface in the kitchen and on a banquet table, when Belinda bustled into the kitchen.

"Good heavens!" she exclaimed. "These cannot be here. The McKinney event is tomorrow. It has to be perfect, Sydney. Absolutely perfect."

"Yes, ma'am," Sydney replied automatically, her fingers stinging under the running water. She was too busy pondering the vase issue to pay much attention to Belinda's excited rambling.

Her ears perked up when she heard, "There will be two girls from the diner working the floor. You'll stay in the kitchen at all times."

Sydney's heart fell, but she said nothing. It was probably for the best. This was Ward's event, and though she desperately wanted to see him, Belinda couldn't find out they knew each other. Sydney wouldn't be able to hide it if she was out amidst the guests. She could find joy in having help for this event. If something went wrong, it would still be her fault somehow, but she wouldn't be trying to do everything on her own.

She realized that Belinda seemed to be expecting an answer, but she had no idea what she'd been asked. "The event will be wonderful. The highlight of the year," she assured Belinda, hoping it was the right thing to say.

"Well, it won't be if this mess doesn't get cleaned up," Belinda gestured to the vases, whirled around, and left the room.

Sydney set the last vase aside to dry and wiped her hands on a towel. She found the event book from the proposal and dug up the contact information for each of the florists. She started calling them, begging them to come back and take their vases. It took longer than she'd hoped, but eventually she had enough commitments to move on. As she prepared the appetizers and desserts for the event, various florists came and went. By the time she had to leave for Black, only a few remained, and she shoved them into a cabinet.

Sydney rushed to Black, despite dreading walking through the door. Tad and Belinda acted as though they hadn't just locked her in the dark for a week, and her work schedule was just as grueling as ever. This shift, she found herself assigned to deep cleaning all night. She did what she could for the first part of the night, but the restaurant was too busy. She spent most of the time cleaning and organizing the dry goods inventory room, the locker room, and the back of the kitchen, away from the activity.

As the food service slowed down and alcohol sales picked up, she started tackling the walk-in fridge and freezer. Containers of undated sauces and meats fermenting and growing mold were much worse than the roses had been. She cleared out container after container and took out multiple bags of trash, running the dishes through the dishwasher as quickly as possible. The chef only barked at her to move three or four times, which she considered a win.

Before she could leave, she had to run the last of the glassware from the evening through the dishwasher and put it away. She thought she was alone in the building, aside from a bartender cleaning up out front and perhaps

Tad. Some nights he stayed until close, and others he didn't. She hadn't found any rhyme or reason to his comings and goings. Ready to leave, she made her way down the hall and paused at the shard of light coming from Tad's office doorway. His voice and booming laughter echoed out into the hall.

"I'm moving up," he said. She could hear the smile in his voice. "I'll be at the event of the year as a *guest*. The son is a prick, but I'll get the old man's ear. I'll be able to sell him on the plan, I'm sure of it. And if I can convince him the son is up to something, all the better. My wife and her kid think he hangs the stars, but I see the entitled, smug SOB he really is. You'll see. You won't be disappointed. Now, can I interest you in a little entertainment? I think we've still got a girl or two around that might fit your tastes."

The creak of his chair jolted Sydney into action. She slipped into the women's bathroom, hoping to go unnoticed. Her heart was pounding, and she reached up to touch the necklace that always brought her comfort before remembering she'd given it away. She swallowed hard and took a few deep breaths. She definitely wasn't supposed to hear that conversation. She wished she'd been able to record it, though. What had Tad been talking about? It'd sounded like he'd been talking about Ward, but he hadn't named any names.

She waited, leaning against the wall, listening for any sounds of movement. She remembered Ice's words about a phone stashed here and opened the cabinet under the sink. She didn't see anything at first, but she felt around and found it adhered to the underside of the counter. She slipped it in her pocket, and when footsteps moved past the bathroom and down the hall, she counted to ten and slipped out, exiting the other direction. She eased the door closed with a soft snick.

She walked as calmly and quickly as she could until she felt she was far enough away to be safe. She ducked just barely into an alley, partly hidden from the street, but not too far into the darkness, and she powered up the phone. Her hands shook enough that she had to take a steadying breath.

It was after two in the morning. She shouldn't call at this hour. She shouldn't wake him up. But she was afraid of forgetting what had been said and afraid of being caught with a phone. The one they'd given her was stashed in the bottom of a bag that she'd never used, in her closet. Now she'd have to hide this one too. She tried to calm herself. If Ward didn't answer, she'd try again tomorrow.

She found his number saved under favorites, alongside Ice and Elle. Two rings later, his sleepy voice answered, "Hello?"

She closed her eyes. "Ward?" she replied, just over a whisper.

He sounded much more alert when he asked, "Sydney? What's wrong?"

She shook her head, even though he couldn't see her. "I'm okay, but I just overheard something that might be important or might be nothing."

"Okay. Are you somewhere safe?"

Sydney looked around. "I don't know. Hopefully. I just left Black. I need to get home. But I don't want anyone to overhear, and I can't be seen on the phone, so I'm in an alley."

"How far are you from the hotel we took you to that first night?" he asked. She could hear rustling on the other end of the line.

Sydney looked around to get her bearings. "Not far. Why?"

"Go there. Don't hang up. Hold on a second." The line went quiet. Sydney walked briskly the few blocks to the hotel. Ward was back before she arrived. "Sorry about that. Where are you?"

"Just walking into the lobby now." The bright lights of the lobby were a sharp contrast to the blackness outside.

"Okay, is there anyone else around?" Through the phone, a door slammed and keys jingled.

She looked around the lobby, seeing no one. "Just the employee at the desk."

"Go up to them and put me on speaker please, Syd."

"Good evening, miss. How may I help you?" the older man at the desk asked politely, his uniform neatly pressed.

She said hi and held her phone out. She didn't have to wonder what to say. Ward took over. "This is Ward McKinney."

"Mr. McKinney, good evening. What can I do for you both?" he repeated his question, his eyebrows lifted in surprise.

"This is my friend Sydney. She had a bit of a scare this evening, and she needs a safe and quiet place to wait. I'm on my way to pick her up and take her home."

"Yes, of course, that's not a problem. Let's go see if there's anyone in the business center, shall we? It should be deserted at this hour." He came around the desk and showed her down the hall to a dark room with a computer and a few tables and seating areas, like a comfortable lounge.

"I trust no one will disturb her, and if anyone asks, you haven't seen her," Ward said with steel in his tone.

"Of course, sir. I have the memory of a goldfish when needed."

"Thank you. Syd, I'll be there in a few minutes." The call ended, and Sydney made her way into the room. She waved to the desk clerk.

"Let me know if you need anything, miss," he said as he returned to the desk.

Sydney turned on a lamp and sat on a couch that looked more comfortable than it was. She thought back over the conversation she'd overheard and tried to make sense of it. Had he been threatening Ward or talking about someone else entirely?

Ward hadn't been kidding when he'd said he'd be there in minutes. Before she knew it, he and Ice walked in, both more disheveled than she'd ever seen them. Ward's hair stood askew, and he was wearing well-worn jeans, a plain white t-shirt that hugged his chest, and a black leather jacket. Ice was in sweats. It took Sydney a moment to absorb that they'd both gotten up in the middle of the night and rushed over here.

"Sorry to wake you both."

Ward sat on the low table in front of her. He took her hands in his, his knees on either side of hers. Ice sat close beside her on the couch, his shoulder brushing hers. Between the two of them, she was enveloped in warmth. Ice picked up the phone from where she'd set it on her lap. "It's fine. I wasn't asleep. I can have this put back. Where did it come from?" he asked, his voice gravely.

"Black, thank you."

"You weren't asleep?" Ward asked, incredulous.

"We're not here to talk about me," Ice redirected, and Sydney smiled at their banter before sobering. Right. They were here because she needed to talk to them.

"What happened, Syd?" Ward asked, warming up her hands between his and leaning close.

"Maybe nothing? Black was closed, and just about everyone had gone home. I heard Tad's voice from his office. I couldn't tell if he was talking to someone on the phone or in person at first, but he was talking about selling something to the 'old man' this weekend at the event of the year and convincing him 'the jerk son' was up to something." Ward's hands stopped moving, and he and Ice exchanged a look. "Do you think he was talking about your event this weekend? Is he planning something against you? Or am I wrong? I don't understand."

"Thank you," Ward said. "He asked to attend the event as a guest when I approved the details. I don't know what he has planned, but it's good to know we need to keep an eye on him. I don't have any dark secrets to uncover. I do have something planned that's going to send him off the deep end, though. I need to fill Dad in on those developments sooner than I'd hoped. I've been holding off until we hear from Ava." His gaze settled on their joined hands. "Let's get you home before he realizes you've been gone too long."

Ice cleared his throat. "Before we go ... Sydney, can we talk about the week you disappeared?"

She shuddered and blinked, stunned silent. No one spoke for a long moment, but Ward kept hold of her hands. "I don't think that's a good idea," she finally answered. She closed her eyes, focusing on the warmth from Ward's hands and Ice's shoulder pressed against hers. Neither responded.

How could she tell them that Belinda and Tad had locked her in the dark and that it was only by luck that there'd been any food or water to keep her alive? That she was walking on eggshells every moment of every day? She couldn't. Ava was more important than anything, and she wasn't safe yet. She looked up, and Ward met her eyes. "We all know that Tad and Belinda are terrible people," she whispered. "Can we just leave it at that? At least until Ava is safe? Please?"

Ice grumbled beside her but stood. "Your safety is important too. Don't go silent like that again." The bite in his tone startled her, but his concern cut through.

She nodded. "I'll try." She certainly planned to be smarter and stash the phone at home in the basement, just in case.

Sydney and Ward stood, and they all walked out to the lobby together. Ward stopped at the front desk and read the clerk's name tag. "Thomas? Thank you for your help. What do you need to ensure no one else knows about this? Sometime soon, it won't be a secret that Sydney and I are friends, but for now, silence is important for her safety."

Thomas waved a hand and gave them a kind smile. "Like I said earlier, sir, memory of a goldfish. I like my job here, and your company is the biggest client we have. I'm not going to do anything to jeopardize that." Ward shook his hand, and they left. Sydney was still stuck on Ward's words. Their friendship wouldn't always be a secret. She looked forward to that day, not because she wanted the attention of everyone in his world, but because she was tired of hiding. She was tired of the fear and the darkness. For now, she could hold that promise in her heart and draw on it when she needed Ward's strength.

The house was dark and the neighborhood quiet when they drove past. Ice parked just down the block, close enough that they could see the front door. Ward squeezed Sydney's hand. She leaned her head against his shoulder, not in a hurry to leave, even though they all knew time was ticking.

"Soon, Sydney," he vowed. He brought her hand up to his lips and kissed it, lingering for a long moment. It wasn't enough. Every time he saw her, it became harder to let her go.

She pulled back and met his gaze, her eyes wide. He wondered what she was thinking. What he wouldn't give for more than a fleeting moment with her. Sydney leaned over and kissed him on the cheek so quickly he didn't see it coming. She slipped out of the car and walked down the sidewalk to the house as if she hadn't just shaken him to his core. He watched Sydney ease the door open and creep inside. The house remained dark and quiet. It was a long moment before Ice put the car back in gear.

"Bold if he thinks he's going to turn your own father against you. What does Tad have against you, anyway?" Ice grumbled, oblivious to the tempest in Ward's mind.

Ward coughed to clear the lump in his throat. His voice still came out little steadier than a croak. "No idea. Tad seems to think he's a player in the big leagues, but he isn't even playing the right sport."

"I'll make sure to schedule extra security this weekend. We might need it."

Ward nodded. He didn't like it. He truly wanted the anniversary party to be just that, a celebration and not an opportunity for chaos or confrontation. He'd try to keep everything civil and let the gloves come off later, but if Tad ruined this event, retribution would be swift.

"So, my friend, who did we tear you away from tonight?" Ward asked to lighten the mood as they pulled into their building's garage.

Ice glanced at him and parked the car. "I'm not answering that."

As he closed his door and they walked to the elevator, Ward replied, "I thought we were friends. You're hiding a relationship from me? Why?"

Ice rolled his eyes. "It's just Jen, Ward. You know her."

"I do. I didn't think it was anything serious. I'm happy for you. She seems nice."

"It isn't serious. We have a good time together. Don't overthink it. Now, though," Ice checked his watch, "I need to try to get a few hours of sleep before work. See you later." He stepped off the elevator onto his floor, leaving Ward alone the rest of the way up.

Ward let himself into his condo and paced. Things were happening, and this weekend would either be incredibly satisfying, or it was all going to go to hell. It was a tossup. Knowing that Tad put a target on his back was a wrench he would adapt to. He thought through what Sydney risked everything to tell him; Tad had to have been talking about him. The only party this weekend that any of the local elites would be attending was his. And Ward certainly fostered the reputation that she had referred to of being a jerk.

Ward forced himself to get some rest, but it was elusive. He stared at the ceiling for most of the night, his mind racing. The weekend couldn't come fast enough.

THE NEXT MORNING, as soon as he stepped off the elevator, Ward approached his dad's assistant. "Is he available?" he asked. She nodded and waved him in.

"Ward! Good morning! What brings you in to see me?" his father greeted him with a one-armed hug. Ward sat, and his father followed suit.

"Do you know Tad Marshall?" he asked, getting right to the point.

Russell steepled his fingers under his chin. "No, I don't think so. Should I?"

Ward shrugged. "He owns a few restaurants and the

Keller Event Center. He seems to think he's important. I'm hearing rumblings that he may be planning to approach you, either to pitch something to you or to convince you that I have done something you'd find distasteful. I don't know what his angle is yet, but whatever he does won't surprise me. I just didn't want you to be blindsided. I do have some plans for his restaurants that don't involve him, but he doesn't know that yet, and we'll need to talk about whether you think I should make that move personally or here with the McKinney Enterprises' support."

His father leaned forward in his chair with a smile on his face. "Tell me more. This sounds personal."

Ward nodded but wasn't sure how much he was ready to share. He kept it general for now. "Like I said, he has several restaurants: the diner on First, the pretentious Walnut Alley on Lakeside, and the equally pretentious bar, Black, in addition to Keller. I like the diner. It does a good amount of business, seems profitable, the staff are good. It would be a good business in any portfolio. Walnut is profitable as well, but just barely. The critics don't even seem to like it. It needs an overhaul. Keller is doing well but is vacant more than it should be." He paused.

"So tell me about Black." His father was still the sharpest guy he knew.

"Black seems to be Tad's baby. He's there more than he's anywhere else. The food is crap, the concept confusing. The drinks are okay. It's a hangout for young professional wannabes and older has-beens." Russell waited for

Ward to continue. "The financials I was able to procure show too much profit. I think he's selling more than food and drink. A friend who works there was harassed by a customer that expected more service, and that's the only way the financials make sense."

"Sex or drugs would be profitable, I suppose, though I'm surprised he'd run that through the business." He tapped his fingers on the desk in thought.

Ward nodded. "I thought so too, but he burned through some sizable loans, and I'm sure he needed to show cash flow to be appealing to his investor."

"Anyone we know?" Russell asked, nodding along.

A wide smile stretched across Ward's face. "Yes, actually. Robert Tate."

Russell burst out in laughter. "Tate? The guy you've been considering taking over? Did all of this come up in that due diligence?"

"Yes and no. It's just serendipitous that I can kill two birds with one stone." He sobered. "But the complications with Black's possible illegal income make me hesitant to bring it to the Board. It might be a risk I should take on personally."

Russell studied him for so long that Ward shifted in his seat. Finally, he asked, "What's really fueling your desire to shove this Marshall out of his businesses? I know Tate is a walking disaster, but this is different. You've never been interested in restaurants. Profit margins suck in food." When Ward didn't answer, his dad slapped his hand down on the desk, startling him. "It's a girl, isn't it? Is there finally a woman who has your attention?"

Ward felt his face warm. He didn't want to go there, but he couldn't lie to his father. "Okay, okay, yes, there is. A friend," he clarified. "Tad Marshall is her stepfather, I guess. It's complicated. He has treated her ..." He searched for appropriate words and gritted his teeth. "He has treated her horribly and exploited her. For *years*. I want him to suffer."

"When can I meet her?" Russell asked, ignoring the vengeance in his son's declaration. A smile lit up his face.

Ward shook his head. "She often works at Keller. I imagine she'll be at this weekend's event, but until she's free of her family, I don't want to draw any attention to our friendship. It's complicated, and it isn't safe for her."

"Okay, I'll be patient. You'll let me know if there's something I can do?" Ward nodded. "It sounds like you have enough information to take it to the board and see what they think. The situation with Black is less than desirable, but I don't see any issue with the rest, depending on the terms. Someone on the board was a restauranteur. Bart, I think. He'll have a good eye for pitfalls."

"Thanks, Dad." Ward rose and left the room with so much on his mind that he didn't notice that Chantelle hadn't shown up for work. He requested time on the agenda for the next board meeting and focused on his presentation. He outlined responses to every objection he could think of. He had to get this right.

A few hours later, Ice walked into his office and gestured toward her desk. "Where's your assistant?"

Ward just blinked and shrugged. "No idea. Haven't heard from her this morning."

Ice tilted his head. "Are you going to call HR to check on her?"

"Hell, no. I don't want to talk to Belinda any more than I want to talk to Chantelle. Maybe she's off doing event crap. I don't really care, Ice." Ice just chuckled and sat across from him. "What are you doing here in the middle of the day? Are we supposed to be somewhere?" Ward asked as he pulled up his calendar. He had a meeting with the director of New Hope and his architect to finalize some of the plans for the new building in a few hours, but it was virtual.

"Nope, just thought I'd stop by. Extra security is arranged for this weekend. Security around here is running like the well-oiled machine that it is. I don't have anything better to do than make you uncomfortable."

"Tell me more about Jen," Ward shot back.

Ice laughed and stood to leave. "She's fun. You should try fun, Ward. It's a nice change. I'll check on your assistant." He left, and Ward went back to work. Fun sounded like a good idea. He would have fun when Sydney could. That was the thought he would hang on to.

"THANK you for fitting me in today. An opportunity has arisen that is a bit outside of our usual projects, but it will add diversification to our portfolio for pennies on the dollar." Ward meticulously detailed the four establishments and their potential for profitability. His presentation was met with stony faces all around the table. The only friendly face was his father's.

Ward's ire rose and he fought to keep his voice calm. "I've brought millions of dollars of profit into this business."

The chairman, Charles Weatherby, leaned back in his chair. "No one questions that. You've earned your position here. But you've also just put the wheels in motion for a philanthropic project. We're here to make money and you've spent enough. Make more and try again. We aren't going to sign off on restaurants. Our answer is no." Heads nodded around the table. Russell stared at Charles, but he didn't back down. "You're excused. We'll look forward to your next profitable project."

Russell slammed his hand on the table and stood. He grabbed Ward by the shoulder and walked out with him. Ward fumed the whole walk to his father's office, his fists clenched. They said no. He wasn't used to hearing no. He'd prepared diligently, answered every objection.

"Ward," his father snapped. He blinked and accepted the drink Russell handed him. The alcohol burned as he swallowed, but it cleared his mind.

"The ducks are in a row," Ward said. "All I have to do is pull the trigger."

"And blow up your position here? Is that really what you want to do?" He leaned against his desk, his expression neutral.

Ward hung his head at the idea of disappointing his father. "It's personal," he admitted. "I know it isn't rational. But I'm not going to lose money on this." Sydney didn't need him to destroy Tad. He wanted to. The opportunity was right there, in his hands. Tad wouldn't see it coming.

"I may not be able to save you, son. Be very sure, whatever you decide."

TWENTY

SYDNEY

Butterflies trapped in a tornado. That's what Sydney felt in her gut as she paced the kitchen at Keller, wiping the counters that already gleamed. Sydney had never been this nervous for an event or a work shift. Everything needed to be perfect, not only because Tad was breathing down her neck about it, but because it was for Ward. This anniversary party was important to him. He was important to her. She would do everything in her power to make the evening perfect.

She ran through the binder one more time. The space was set up just right, and all of the food was ready to go. Even though she was banished to the kitchen, she straightened her uniform and made sure her hair was presentable.

Just before guests were supposed to arrive, Leah arrived ready to work. Mindy from Black hadn't shown up yet, but Sydney expected she would. Sydney didn't know her well, but she was always on the schedule to work.

Tad walked into the kitchen and clapped his hands to get their attention, as if they hadn't both turned to face him when he'd entered. "Today's the day!" his voice boomed. He frowned and scanned the kitchen. "Where is the third employee?" Sydney and Leah just looked at each other. How would they know? "I scheduled two to be out front and Sydney in the kitchen."

Sydney sighed. She'd already known that was where she was supposed to be, but it still grated on her nerves. Just this once, she'd like to be able to see Ward and his family together in their element. She'd never fit in. She knew that. But it could be fun to dream.

Tad grumbled, his face red and sweat on his brow. "I have to go change. You two will make sure everything is ready. No screw-ups tonight. Understand?" When they nodded, he whirled around and stormed down the hall.

Sydney shook off Tad's attitude and focused on the task at hand. "I'm glad you're here, Leah. It's really nice to work with a friend." She hoped her assumption of friendship wasn't out of line and was relieved when Leah smiled and hugged her.

"It's good to see you, Sydney. I've missed you."

"I've been here the last few days. I hope tonight goes perfectly." She caught herself before expressing her admiration for the guests of honor and their family.

"It's supposed to be a 'who's who' kind of event, from what I understand. What do you need me to do?"

Sydney was surprised by the question. "You haven't

been given any instructions?" she clarified. Leah shook her head. "Oh, well, you and Mindy are supposed to be working the event space, circulating with the appetizers, getting guests anything they need, that sort of thing. Make sure if someone spills, it gets cleaned up right away." She pulled the binder over and showed Leah the time schedule and the menu.

"So basically, just do my job in a fancier setting. Got it."

"Exactly." Sydney smiled.

They were staging the first appetizers when there was a light knock on the doorframe. Sydney looked up and couldn't stop the big smile that spread across her face. "Mr. McKinney," she greeted Ward formally, mindful that Leah was in the room and Tad could be around any corner.

"Good evening, ladies," he replied warmly. His tux fit him perfectly, and Sydney was reminded again that he was part of a different world. The way he looked at her, though, made her feel like it didn't matter. "I just wanted to check in on the preparations. I have complete confidence in you, but indulge me. Tell me everything is on track?"

Her heart warmed at the slight evidence of his nerves. "Yes, everything is ready to go. I'm sure it will be a wonderful evening."

He nodded. "Thank you in advance for all of your hard work. I appreciate it." They heard voices, and Ward turned back to the door. "Here we go," he muttered, heading out to greet his guests.

Leah watched him go with a small smile on her face. "Girl …"

"Don't," Sydney stopped her. A matchmaking sparkle gleamed in Leah's eye. "Please."

"Just one thing," Leah whispered, leaning close. "He and his friend were asking about you, not long ago. It would be colossally dumb to pass him up if he asked you out."

What could she say to that? "I know," Sydney conceded. "Off you go. Go feed the pretty people and make them happy."

Leah grabbed a tray and left the kitchen with a big customer service smile on her face. Mindy rushed in just as Leah walked out. Whatever she'd been doing before she walked in the door, it hadn't been getting ready for work. Her hair was loose in poofy, uncontrolled waves, and her uniform shirt was unbuttoned to an indecent level.

She started to grab a tray, but Sydney stopped her. "Wait! I'm so glad you're here, but you might want to take a minute to breathe and put yourself together before Tad sees you. He's on a rampage about perfection tonight." Sydney had no problem blaming her pickiness on Tad. It was true enough. Mindy looked like she was going to argue, but she left the tray and walked out, hopefully to fix herself up in the restroom.

Sydney set up the rest of the appetizer trays. A few minutes later, Leah came back in with a spring in her step. She swapped her empty tray for a fresh one. "Weren't we supposed to have help?"

A sigh escaped from Sydney's lips. "Mindy was just here. She was a mess, so hopefully she's just putting herself in order. If she walked back out ..." Sydney shuddered to think of Tad's reaction.

Leah looked back and forth between the doorway and Sydney, tray in hand. "There are a lot of guests out there, Syd. One person circulating isn't enough. Maybe we need to put food out on the banquet tables?"

Sydney shook her head. "The instructions explicitly say that guests are to be served tonight, not to serve themselves." She pulled her shoulders back and made a decision. "I'll go check the restroom, and if she isn't there, I'll help you." Leah nodded in relief and went back out.

Sydney marched down to the restroom. Mindy had been gone too long. Sydney prayed she was just having a particularly hard time with her hair or something. The last thing she wanted was a problem this early in the evening, or at all.

The bathroom was empty. So empty that the automatic lights were off when she opened the door. Sydney breathed deeply and stalked back to the kitchen. She could follow Tad's instructions and stay in the kitchen all night, or she could help make sure guests were taken care of. The decision was easy. She had to go out there. She grabbed a tray from the kitchen, put a smile on her face, and circulated the room, offering food as invisibly as possible.

She relaxed as she spotted Ward, of course, and Ice. Elle and Rick raved about the food and said hello. She tensed up again when Tad and Belinda made an exaggerated entrance. Not one attendee paid them any attention. Sydney tried to stay as far from them as possible, and she was grateful that Leah drew their attention her way.

There was commotion as the guests of honor arrived, and the room erupted in applause. Sydney smiled at the confused and embarrassed looks on the faces of Mr. and Mrs. McKinney. Ward tapped a glass and stood with a microphone on the raised platform at the edge of the room.

"Good evening, everyone. Thank you for being here. Dad, Lisa, please join me?"

With everyone focused on Ward, Sydney backed away to refill her tray and minimize distractions for the guests. Leah followed suit.

Ward continued, addressing the guests, "Thank you all for coming to celebrate the anniversary of my dad and his very patient wife." They both gaped at him, hand in hand at his side. At their reaction, he explained, "I should explain that I had a little help and didn't tell them that this event was to honor them. Not only that, I've been a less than ideal son for the last five years. Lisa, thank you for putting up with my blindness and stubbornness. I see now just how good you two are together, and I wish you many, many good years to come."

Shouts of agreement and clinking glasses sounded through the room. Ward's father shrugged and took the microphone. He took a breath to speak, looked at Ward, and shook his head with a smile. His other hand gripped his wife's. Sydney thought she saw his eyes glint with tears, and her heart swelled. He cleared his throat, and the room was silent, waiting for his response.

"You all knew about this?" he asked the crowd, and everyone laughed. "It's not easy to keep secrets when you work as closely together as we do. This is something." He shook his head again. "Thank you, Ward. And thank you all for being here. I'm the luckiest man alive," he declared. "Enjoy yourselves!" He put the microphone down, and Sydney and Leah slipped back into the crowd, circulating food. The bartenders Tad hired were keeping busy.

Sydney checked her watch and ducked into the kitchen in time to change over the appetizers for the main course. She plated meals as quickly as she could, but she knew Tad was going to say something about how slowly food was going out. Leah took out tray after tray as quickly as Sydney filled them. When someone came in to take a tray right after Leah left, Sydney sped up. She looked up and jumped when she recognized Elle had appeared by her side.

"Don't stop." Elle laughed. "Let's get these people fed." She watched Sydney fix up a plate and then jumped right in to help. Food was flying out of the kitchen, and Tad hadn't burst in to make a scene. She counted that as a win. As soon as the last plates went out, empty ones started coming back, and they moved on to plating desserts. An hour passed in a blur to the sound-track of happy voices.

When the last dessert dishes went out and Leah returned, they all took a deep breath. "Thank you for jumping in like that," Leah said. "Where did you even come from? You're too dressed up to be called in by Tad."

Elle laughed. "No, I'm just a friend of the family. It seemed like you were a little shorthanded, and I wanted to make sure everything went smoothly. I've heard Ward has been stressing about this event all week. It was surprisingly thoughtful of him to do this."

"Did I hear my name?" he asked, joining them. He didn't seem to expect an answer. "It's going better than I could have hoped, thanks to all of you."

Elle grinned up at him and gave him a hug. "It was our pleasure. Anything else you need help with, Sydney?" she asked.

Sydney shook her head. "Nah, the rest of the evening should be just cleanup. Thank you. Enjoy the rest of the party." Elle waved and left.

Leah excused herself as well, muttering something about gathering dishes. The volume of the music increased, and Sydney figured the dancing part of the evening had begun. Ward was still standing there, watching her, his hands in his pockets.

"Thank you, Syd," he said in a low, sincere voice. She shrugged. "Don't do that. I know how hard you work. I know how much went into getting everything right for tonight. I appreciate it." He put a hand over his heart.

"You're welcome," she whispered. "You need to get back out there to your guests."

He shrugged and stepped closer, into her personal space. She didn't pull away. He leaned close enough to press a cheek to her hair but kept his hands to himself.

She wanted to reach out and hug him, but she held herself back. "They're my dad's guests. I'm just the one that got them here. I want ..." he trailed off. She closed her eyes and waited, hoping he'd finish his sentence. After a long moment, he continued, "I want to take you out there and introduce you to him. I want to dance with you. And I'm irrationally angry with Tad that I can't ask you to do those things with me."

"Thank you," she replied.

He chuckled and pulled back enough to look into her eyes. "Not the response I was expecting. Why are you thanking me?"

"I want to be free to do those things with you too. I'm glad I'm not alone. Now please go before Tad notices you're missing."

Ward nodded and backed away. As soon as he left the kitchen, Leah burst in with a tray full of empty dessert plates. Sydney started washing dishes and was grateful that Leah hadn't said anything. She couldn't talk about her feelings for Ward, but if Leah's knowing glances were any indication, it was obvious.

In a lull, Sydney slipped down the hall to the restroom but stopped in her tracks when she heard Belinda and Tad yelling at each other in Tad's office. She retreated back out to the party and scanned the room. Ice was nearby, a drink in his hand. He could help. He nodded to her as she approached but didn't greet her, mindful of the room full of people.

She leaned toward him and quietly informed him, "Tad and Belinda are yelling at each other, loudly, in the office. I don't know what they're fighting about, but I'd hate for guests to hear it." She shifted. "I can't go in there and stop them."

He handed her his drink before she finished her sentence. Sydney watched as he retrieved Ward, and they both headed down the hall. Sydney returned to the kitchen and paced. She wanted to know what was happening, but she couldn't risk getting in the middle of it. Soon, Leah rushed into the kitchen, short of breath.

"Is everything okay?" Sydney asked her.

"I think so, but there was a shouting match in the hallway. Tad's wife was escorted out of the building!"

Sydney blinked, not sure she'd heard Leah correctly. "Belinda was removed? She and Tad were yelling at each other. It was unprofessional, but I wouldn't have guessed she'd be the one to go."

Leah shrugged. "Tad's the boss. He has to stay."

"I guess," Sydney agreed, putting the last of the washed dinner plates on the counter. Leah picked up a towel and started drying them.

"You should take a break," Leah encouraged.

Sydney shook her head. "Thanks, but I'm fine. I took a breather while you were out gathering dishes." Leah eyed her skeptically, but she let it go and worked steadily through drying the stack of plates while Sydney moved on to washing the dessert plates. She looked up when Ice popped his head in.

"Everything okay in here, ladies?" he asked.

Sydney's eyebrows rose. "Sure. Everything okay out there?" she replied.

"It is, but please be careful when you leave tonight. One of us can walk you out, or at least be sure to walk out together, okay?"

Leah chirped, "Okay!" and Ice slipped out before Sydney had the chance to question it. Surely he didn't think that Belinda was a threat to anyone outside of the building? She took a break from washing and stepped out cautiously to survey the guests and see how the evening was going. The party was still going strong, with music playing and alcohol flowing. Everything seemed to be in order. She didn't see Tad or the guest of honor anywhere, but she spotted the rest of the familiar faces she expected to find.

She swept through the room picking up glasses, surreptitiously watching the beautiful and glamorous people dancing and happy. A woman was trying to get Ward's attention, and he was ignoring her with a scowl on his face. Ice leaned against the far wall, and at first Sydney thought he was relaxed, but on a second glance, he was just as tense as Ward and as watchful as ever. Elle and Rick seemed genuinely happy dancing together. Their joy made Sydney happy as she finished out her work for the night.

TWENTY-ONE
WARD

The evening had been going so well. Too well, Ward supposed. The shouting match between Tad and Belinda was just the beginning of the slide downhill. He and Ice shut that down, reminding them of their audience.

Tad immediately stepped back and shut up. Belinda continued yelling, turning her ire toward their intrusion into the argument. Ward hid his amusement that Belinda had taken the bait. In her tirade, she'd defended Chantelle and insisted to Tad that the timing might not be right. Ward knew exactly what she was referring to. It was clear as day that Chantelle had dutifully passed along the misinformation that Ward let slip. They'd thought that the announcement that he was branching off to start his own company would have been made at this event.

Ward would have been more amused if they weren't disrupting an otherwise perfect celebration. He was happy to see his dad and Lisa having a good time and being honored by their friends. Even Tate was behaving himself. He'd arrived quietly and was socializing and staying out of trouble. After the dust settled and they kicked Belinda out, Tad returned to mingling under Ice's watchful eye. Ward found it interesting that Tad and Robert never conversed despite their partnership on paper.

As the evening wore on, Ward was ready to call it a night. The downside to hosting was staying until the end. Russell and Lisa were making the rounds, saying their goodbyes, so at least the party was winding down. Once the guests of honor were gone, there was no reason he couldn't shut down the rest.

He saw Ice stalking across the room from the corner of his eye and tracked his path. Tad had Russell cornered and was standing much too close, talking and gesturing wildly. To his credit, Russell didn't flinch. Ice shoved Tad back and stood between them while Tad continued to gesticulate. Two other security guards appeared and removed Tad from the room, yelling louder the closer they got to the door. Ward stayed out of the way and watched as his Dad and Lisa were safely escorted out.

That wasn't the way the evening was supposed to end for the guests of honor. Ward was anxious to find out exactly what Tad wanted so badly that he'd risk making a scene for. He hadn't even glanced Ward's way before storming off with security. Ward itched to follow him, to confront him, but it wasn't a good idea. Not with the influential attendees in the room. Ward remained on his best behavior, thanking people for coming and sending them on their way.

An hour later, all of the guests had gone home, and the remnants of the party were cleaned up. Ward and Ice swept through the building, making sure there weren't any stragglers hiding out. When they returned to the kitchen, Leah, Sydney, and Elle were passing around a container of cookies.

Sydney held it out to him. "For the road?"

He wasn't about to turn down the offering. He took two with a smile. Ice took the whole container, and Ward was mesmerized by Sydney's laughter and the joyful crinkle at the corner of her eyes. He almost reached out to hug her but stopped himself at the last second and swallowed hard. Exhaustion was making it difficult to remember why he should keep his hands to himself.

"Sydney, can I give you a ride home?" Leah asked. Ward bristled. It was for the best, and as long as she had a safe ride, he wouldn't complain, even if it felt wrong to let her go with anyone else.

"That would be great, thanks!" Sydney tucked the last stack of plates into the cabinet.

"I'll go get the car warmed up," Leah said. "Take your time wrapping up." She winked at Sydney on her way out.

Ice followed her, leaving Ward alone with Sydney in the silent kitchen. They didn't have much time, but every moment with her fed his soul. Mindful of the cameras, Ward kept his hands in his pockets while he waited for Sydney to retrieve her sweater. His breath hitched. *His* sweater. Possessiveness hit him like a fist to the chest. Not for the fabric hanging on Sydney's small frame. He had countless more at home. It was the strong, competent woman beneath, who now looked fragile drowning in fabric, who drew this possessiveness from him.

They walked to the main door, flipping light switches off along the way. As they reached the door, Ward's phone buzzed with a text from Ice.

> Paparazzi are still here.

It wasn't lost on Ward that the media attention he had craved and pursued no longer felt important. The last thing he wanted now was to draw their attention to Sydney. Ward reached over Sydney's shoulder and pressed his hand to the door, stopping her from opening it. She started to turn back, but he stopped her with a hand to her waist. "Syd ..." he said, his voice barely above a whisper. When no additional words came, his hand fisted in the sweater at her waist. "It looks good on you," he said.

"It doesn't smell like you anymore," Sydney whispered.

He wrapped his arms around her for just a moment, breathing deeply. He absorbed the peace that he felt around her for just one more moment. He cleared his throat and pulled back. "Paparazzi's outside," he said. "After you lock up, go straight to the car. If they give you any trouble, Ice will intervene." He wanted to say more. He wanted to tell her how he felt about her, but it wasn't the right time. He knew it wasn't the right time. So he pulled back another half a step and let her open the door.

Flashbulbs blinded Ward the moment he stepped out. He guided the photographers to the side. "Gentlemen, nothing better to do this evening?" He kept an eye on Sydney as she locked up and beelined for Leah's car.

The two photographers that remained snapped a few more pictures. One shouted, "You're alone again tonight? What's wrong with you, McKinney? How am I supposed to pay my rent without pics of your flavor of the night?"

Ward grinned for their benefit and slipped into the confident persona he'd been showing the media for years. "Isn't this even better? Your tabloids can speculate all they want about why I've been solo. Maybe ..." He leaned closer and dropped his voice as Leah's car left the lot. "Maybe I'm in a relationship and I've been hiding it." He laughed at their stunned expressions. "Have a good night," he called as he passed them and joined Ice at his idling car.

Once home, the details of the night rushed through his head. His dad's surprise and pride. Lisa's soft, understanding smile. Sydney's support. How it felt to tell the paparazzi he was in a relationship. It felt true and right, even if it wasn't real. Yet. He tried to focus on the good and leave the earlier drama to ponder later. He was mostly successful as he drifted off to sleep.

THE NEXT DAY, Ward was surprised by a call from his dad.

"Ward, do you have a few minutes to talk?" Russell asked.

"Sure, Dad. What's up?"

He could envision his father sitting back in his chair, settling in for a conversation in the pause before he said, "I wanted to thank you again for last night. That was sneaky, and unexpected, and delightful."

Ward's breath rushed out in a whoosh. "Just a few hiccups, but hopefully no one noticed. You and Lisa deserved some love from your friends and family."

"The only hiccup I saw was the one when we were leaving. It's a shame that such a wonderful event center is owned by such an arrogant, manipulative slimeball."

Ward chuckled in surprise at his dad's ire. "What did he want, anyway?"

Russell tsked. "He wanted to convince me that you should be removed from the company and that he had evidence of some unsavory transactions you were party to. I trust there isn't anything I need to know."

"If he comes up with some sort of evidence, it's forged or AI generated. I'm perfectly content making money legally and staying out of trouble."

"That's what I figured. I don't think anyone would doubt you. Tad's a small tadpole in an ocean."

Ward laughed. "I don't think that's quite the saying, but I understand."

"I assume you've made a decision." When Ward didn't reply, he sighed. "I'm proud of you, Ward. See you at work tomorrow." He hung up, leaving Ward feeling warm inside. Those words meant a lot to him.

Ward's fingers hesitated only a moment as he sent a message to his attorney, instructing him to act on the contracts that would remove all of Tad's power. It was risky. He could be throwing away everything he'd worked for. But he wouldn't regret this. Making money was something he was good at. If the firm let him go, he'd strike off on his own and start over.

He had just pressed send when his phone rang again. He didn't recognize the number.

"Hello?" he answered, ready to end the call if it was a telemarketer. The line was silent long enough that he almost hung up, but he waited and repeated himself.

"Um, hi," a girl's voice finally came through the line.

Ward jumped up out of his chair, tipping it backward to clatter on the floor. "Ava?" he whispered, cleared his throat, and then repeated himself.

"Yes. Do you really know my sister?" she asked.

"Yes. She's been so worried about you. In case we get disconnected, which school are you attending?" Ward's heart raced.

"Evergreen Prep Academy. I don't understand what's happening. Why did she ask me to call you? Can I talk to her?"

Ward sighed and wiped a hand down his face. "We'll make that happen, but she's not here with me. Tad and Belinda don't allow her to have a phone. They wouldn't tell her where you are. I'd like to come visit you and your principal or headmaster, and then I'll arrange for Sydney to visit you."

She was quiet for a minute, and she whispered, "I have to go. You'll find me?"

"Count on it. Thanks for calling, Ava."

When she disconnected, Ward needed a minute. His heart was trying to burst out of his chest. She'd called. They knew where she was. He was back in front of his computer and googling the phone number she'd called from even as he was texting Ice. Within moments, he had the location and official phone number of the school. Nothing on his Monday morning agenda was more important than making sure that Ava was safe and secure.

The rest of the day crawled by, and Ward filled it in the gym downstairs. When he couldn't run any more, he tried to distract himself with movies. He'd thought he was a patient man, but he was seriously struggling to wait until morning to move forward.

The moment the school opened in the morning, Ward was on the phone from his home office with Ice sitting across from him. In minutes, he had an appointment for later that morning. The school was over an hour away, but that didn't deter either of them.

Walking into the school reminded him of his own prep school days, with students in uniforms rushing from class to class. He and Ice found the office easily enough and waited for the headmaster to be ready for them.

"Does every school look the same?" Ice muttered. They weren't kept waiting long and were shown into a pristine office, with nothing out of place and no paper in sight. The headmaster was a serious woman wearing a dark suit. Her hair was swept up in a tight bun.

"Good morning, gentlemen. I'm aware of who you are, Mr. McKinney, and I'm curious why you're here at my school." She gestured for them to sit across from her as she eased into her desk chair. Ice remained standing near the door.

"Don't mind him," Ward explained. "He's security. I'm here to talk about one of your students. I understand I am not an authorized person, so I'd like to request that she be called in to talk with us. But first, I have a very important request."

She was leaning back in her chair and frowning at him. "Go on," she prompted.

Assured of her attention, Ward continued, "I'm sure we can agree that the most important thing here is that this student is safe." He waited for her to nod. "There are circumstances at home that you are not aware of, and while I don't expect you to trust me, I need to know that this conversation will not leave this room. There will not be a phone call or carrier pigeon home to her guardians. Again, her safety is my priority, and I'm willing to donate a significant sum to this school to ensure her safety isn't compromised."

"I understand. This is highly unusual. I suppose as long as I don't see any indication that you're here to harm her, there won't be anything for me to report home."

"If you wouldn't mind calling her in, I'll explain more with her in the room. Her first name is Ava. Her last name is Harrett, but she may be registered as Marshall."

She narrowed her eyes but made the call for Ava Harrett to come to the office. They waited in tense silence for several minutes. When she peeked into the room and Mrs. Allard waved her in, she took one look at Ward and threw her arms around him, shocking him. He would've recognized her anywhere. She was younger but looked strikingly like Sydney. "Hi, Ava."

"Have a seat, Miss Harrett," Mrs. Allard commanded. She immediately complied, wiping tears from her face. She looked around the room, took in Ice, and returned her gaze to Ward.

"Is Sydney here?" she asked.

Ward shook his head. "Not today. I wanted to make sure you were safe and everything was good here first. I'll explain to catch both of you up." He addressed Mrs. Allard. "When Ava was little, the girls' father died. He had remarried, so they stayed with their stepmother, Belinda. When she remarried Tad Marshall, Ava was sent here. The girls have not been allowed to see or talk to each other aside from monthly letters that are sometimes confiscated, and Sydney hasn't known where Ava is until now. Sydney is older than Ava, and she was kept at home and forced to work in their businesses to pay for Ava's tuition."

At Ava's gasp, he turned toward her. "You are the most important person in Sydney's life. She's been doing everything in her power to make sure you had a good education here, away from the Marshalls. But as you're getting older and approaching graduation, she's been worried about Tad and Belinda's priorities and what they'll do next."

Ava's tears silently streaked down her cheeks. "I thought she'd forgotten me," she whispered.

"Not for a single moment, Ava." He turned back to Mrs. Allard. "I have to request again that the Marshalls not be informed of our visit, and if anyone aside from myself or Ice," he gestured behind them, "who handles my security, asks about Ava that we be informed immediately. Tad's illegal activities are coming to light. There are some things that are about to go very wrong for the Marshalls, and I don't want Ava to suffer if they lash out, as they've threatened to do. I'll do everything I can to help Sydney petition for guardianship until Ava turns eighteen, but the courts take a long time and may not act fast enough."

"I understand," she replied. Her frown had turned into a small, compassionate smile as she took in Ava's tears. "I imagine you have questions for Mr. McKinney, here. Unless there's anything else you need from me, I will go do my rounds to give you privacy, if you're comfortable with that, Ava?" At her nod, Mrs. Allard rose from her chair. Ward and Ava rose as well. "I can give you about a half hour. My office manager is just outside this door." Ward heard her implication. If Ava felt unsafe, help was just on the other side of the door. He wasn't offended.

"There is actually one more thing." Ward stopped her from leaving. "Has Ava's tuition been paid through the end of the school year, or are there any outstanding charges? If there is a balance and the Marshalls default, please notify me, and I'll take care of it. Don't send her away."

She nodded and tapped on her keyboard. After few moments, she confirmed, "There are still two payments left for the term, but I'll make a note that her fees are guaranteed."

"Thank you."

Mrs. Allard locked her computer and left the room.

"Tell me about Sydney," Ava pleaded.

Ward shook his head. "I'm just getting to know her myself. She looks just like you, and she's selfless and brave and determined. And I'll bring her to meet you as soon as I can."

"Was she really not getting my letters?"

"She's been getting some, but it sounds like Belinda hasn't been mailing hers back to you."

"Why are they so mean? What did we ever do to them?" Ava asked in a small voice, twisting her hands together.

Ward covered her hands with his. "It will come back to bite them. Karma is real," he assured her.

"I'm scared," she confided. "I don't have anywhere to go after graduation. I haven't gotten any acceptance letters, at least not with enough scholarships to go."

"I don't know the future, Ava. I do know that your sister will do anything to make sure you have a home and everything you need to figure out what's next. And she's not alone. She has me, and Ice, and our families to help."

She was quiet for a minute. Finally, she asked, "If you

have security with you, you must be someone important?"

Ice chuckled behind them, and she turned to look at him. "What's funny?" she asked.

They shook their heads. "Nothing," Ward answered. "I am well known in the business community, and there are threats against me now and then. He's also my best friend." They stood as the bell rang, indicating Ava should return to class.

Ava hugged Ward again, and he fought the emotion that choked him. She asked, "You'll look out for Sydney?"

"Yes," they both answered, making her smile.

"It was nice to meet you. Tell Sydney I'm okay and give her a hug for me?"

"You can count on it," Ward assured her. "Stay out of trouble, okay?"

Ava nodded and walked out of the room with a bounce in her step. When she was out of sight, Ice asked, "You aren't actually going to tell Sydney we saw her today, are you?"

Ward sighed. "Not yet. But soon."

TWENTY-TWO
SYDNEY

When Sydney arrived at Black on Friday afternoon, the restaurant was abuzz. Signs on the front door and in the locker room stated that the restaurant would be closed for the following three days. Employees clustered in groups, wondering aloud if the restaurant was closing for good. Details were included for an all-employee meeting to be held at Keller Event Center Tuesday morning. No one was encouraged when shift managers just shrugged and said they didn't know anything. No one had seen Tad all week, including Sydney.

Once customers started arriving, everyone settled in to work, and the chatter quieted down. Sydney fell into the familiar rhythm of washing dishes and tuned everyone out. The restaurant closing could be a bad thing, but she wasn't going to dwell on it. Instead, she hoped it meant she'd have three days off from this place. She was tired of being on edge. Tad's absence had been a blessing, but it was almost more nerve wracking not knowing where he was and when he'd reappear.

Two hours into her shift, she heard a familiar voice behind her. "Miss Harrett, would you come with me, please?" The kitchen fell silent for a moment. No one here had ever shown her as much respect as Ice just had. She turned to face him and took in his usual pristine suit and natural air of authority. No wonder no one questioned his presence. "Is there anything you need from the back before leaving?" he asked. She nodded, and he nodded back. "I'll wait."

Sydney grabbed Ward's hoodie and returned in moments. Ice gestured to the door and guided her out with a light touch on her back. In the hallway, two massive men in suits stood outside Tad's office, and Sydney shrank against the wall.

"They're with me, Syd. It's okay," Ice assured her. When they reached the door to the restroom, he stopped her. "Just a minute." He opened the door and looked inside, calling out to make sure no one was inside. He handed Sydney a large gift bag and said, "You may wish to change. If this doesn't fit, or you don't like it, what you're wearing is fine. I'll be right here, and no one will disturb you. Take your time."

Sydney was so confused. She tentatively took the bag from him but didn't move. "What's going on?" she whispered.

"Trust me. Trust Ward. We do need to get going, though." He nudged her into the restroom.

Sydney stepped inside and opened the gift bag, finding a letter on top.

> Sydney,
>
> We haven't met yet. I'm on family medical leave right now, but I'm Ward's assistant, Marian. Ward has never once asked me to do something personal, so I'm honored he asked for my help with this. I hope the dress fits and is flattering. If not, I apologize and can only blame the dreadfully vague information he was able to give me. I'll do better next time, and I hope there will be a next time. Ward seemed softer and kinder somehow, when I talked with him this week, and I can only assume that's your doing. I hope you have a lovely evening and look forward to meeting you.
>
> Marian

Sydney blinked, put the letter back in the bag, and pulled out a sage dress. It was the prettiest thing she'd had to wear in forever. She quickly shed her black uniform and slipped the dress over her head. It fit with just enough give that she had room to breathe and move. The cozy fabric, long sleeves, and ankle length would keep her warm. Next, she found off-white ankle boots with a small, chunky heel. When she folded up her uniform to add to the bag, she found a pair of warm tights as well and slipped them on.

Once dressed, she put the boots on and looked in the mirror. Her cheeks were pink, and a new excitement shone in her eyes. She didn't know what it meant that Ice had brought her a dress and was here to take her away, but she trusted him. She tried to tame her hair and took a deep breath. She was as ready as she'd ever be for whatever awaited her.

She stepped out to find Ice waiting patiently. He took the bag from her and handed it off to someone behind him. He held out a long, off-white, wool coat and scarf for her to slip into. Warm, comfortable, and feeling like a new person, she smiled. Ice took her hand and tucked it into his arm and started them moving toward the door. No one she worked with even did a double take as she walked through the restaurant to the door.

Once outside, the back door of a black SUV with dark windows was opened, and Ice urged her inside. He sat up front with the driver, and the bag with her clothes was placed in the back before the vehicle moved away from the curb.

"What's going on?" she asked, nerves fluttering in her chest.

"Ward will be meeting us there. It's a bit of a drive. Relax, Syd. Everything is okay," he assured her in a calm voice.

Sydney tried to take his advice. All of her concerns

about the last couple of hours were swirling around in her mind, but soon, the gentle motion of the vehicle and white noise of traffic lulled her to sleep.

She awoke to cool air rushing in and Ice gently telling her it was time to wake up. She blinked to clear the sleep from her mind. She turned and took the hand he offered to help her from the tall SUV. "Where are we?" she asked, looking up at the entrance of what looked like a restaurant.

"Dinner," he replied simply, escorting her inside. At first, it appeared to be deserted. Ice nodded to the employee at the front and walked Sydney directly through to a table in the back where she recognized Ward with relief. It only took a moment to realize he wasn't alone. He was helping another woman remove her jacket. Sydney's smile wavered, but then she looked closer and stopped in her tracks. Ice squeezed her shoulder and waited.

"Ava?" she whispered, not believing her eyes.

"Go hug your sister," Ice whispered back. He didn't need to tell her twice.

She rushed forward and cried, "Ava!" as she reached them. She only hesitated for a moment, waiting for Ava's response, before she crushed her sister in a hug. Tears streamed down both of their faces. Sydney couldn't believe she was real. She pulled back and wiped the tears from Ava's face and studied her. It was like looking in a mirror. "You found her," she croaked out, looking around for Ward and Ice, who were hovering close.

Ward helped Sydney with her coat. He pulled out a

chair for her, as Ice did for Ava, and they sat around a table. They were the only guests in the room.

Ward noticed her unasked question and explained, "I thought you two would want privacy to catch up," as if it was the most normal thing in the world to pay for a restaurant to close for you. Maybe it was a normal thing for him. She'd have to ask about that later. For now, her sister was here, and she didn't want to miss a moment with her. "Would you prefer we leave you alone?" Ward asked as a waiter approached.

Sydney grabbed his hand and looked to Ava for her response. "Stay," Ava chirped. "For now, anyway. Later, I might want to ask her about you." She smiled, and Sydney laughed, even as she cried over the idea of having girl talk with her sister.

"You okay?" Ward whispered near her ear, sending shivers down her spine.

Sydney nodded but couldn't take her eyes off her sister. The waiter rattled off the specials and asked if they wanted something to drink. Sydney wasn't paying attention. Ava was here, and she looked healthy and happy. She couldn't ask for anything more. The waiter returned with waters for all of them and a root beer for Ava.

She blushed and took a sip. "We don't get soda at school," she admitted.

"I want to know everything," Sydney whispered, struggling to find her voice. "I've missed so much."

Ava shrugged. "Not really. It's just school, sitting in class all day, listening to teachers, writing papers. Your life must be more exciting. Tell me about you!"

Sydney laughed. "My life isn't exciting either. I wash dishes at a couple of Tad's restaurants, wait tables sometimes at the diner, and do catering and setup for events. The events can be special, to see everyone all glammed up in tuxes and beautiful dresses." Ward squeezed her hand. "Sometimes the people in charge of the events are demanding and awful. Sometimes they're wonderful," she added, thinking about Ward's event. "Do you have dances? Parties?"

The waiter came back to take their meal orders. Sydney still hadn't even considered the menu. Ward leaned toward her. "How does chicken fettuccini sound?"

She nodded. "That sounds great, thank you." He confirmed the order, and Ava said, "Me too." Once their orders were in, Ava fiddled with her straw.

"Ava?" Sydney asked, gently, wondering about her mood shift. Ava had been so perky since they'd arrived. "What's wrong?"

Ava swallowed hard. "I don't fit in at school," she admitted. "There are parties. More than the administration knows about. I'm just not invited to them."

"Why not?"

"Because they're all snobs?" Ava ranted. "They're awful. All they care about is their Ivy League futures and their trust funds. I'm not one of them. They say I'm a scholarship kid and I don't belong. That I'll never be anything. And the colleges seem to agree. Not one acceptance letter, Syd. Not even one. And I haven't been applying to the top schools, just local ones. I don't understand what's wrong with me. Why do people have to be so awful?"

Sydney's heart broke, and she pulled Ava into a hug. She felt Ward's hand on her back, lending her support. "I wish I'd known, Ava. I'm so sorry. People suck." She squeezed her sister tighter. If only she'd known that Ava was as miserable as she was. "I've been trying to do the right thing. Trying to make sure you had everything you needed to survive without Tad and Belinda."

Ava eased back and wiped her eyes. "It's not your fault people suck, Syd. Are people nicer to you?"

Sydney shuddered. "No. They're not. These two are, though. I'm not sure how I got lucky enough to find them."

Ward cleared his throat. "You only need a couple of good people in your life to offset the bad ones."

"I hope that's true," Ava replied as their food arrived.

Sydney wasn't hungry, but the food smelled good. She wound some pasta around her fork and took a bite of the best meal she'd ever eaten. She savored the rich, creamy sauce and tender chicken. She looked up and found Ward watching her. She wiped her face with her napkin. "Did I get it everywhere?" she asked. He shook his head but didn't look away.

Sydney smiled at him, happy to be here, happy to spend time with people she cared about, savoring good food. She turned back to Ava and asked, "What kinds of things do you like to do? I feel like our letters have been so sanitized for Belinda, I don't know what was true and what was just easy to write."

Ava cringed. "That's fair. I read a lot. The library is my favorite place on campus."

"Any types of books in particular?"

"Nope. I love them all. Fiction, non-fiction, all genres, it doesn't matter. I'd like to be an author or a librarian, or work in a bookshop. Or write while working at a bookshop."

"That sounds like a great plan," Sydney said with a smile.

"What about you?" Ava asked. "Do you want to do something other than what you're doing now?"

Ward leaned forward and set his fork down. Sydney took another bite while she considered the question. "I don't know," she replied honestly. "I've never considered what I would do if I got to choose for myself. There are things I like about what I do. I like waiting tables at the diner. One of the other waitresses is really nice. I like finding new recipes and making something different for catering events. Especially desserts."

Ice had been quiet, but he piped up, "Please make those strawberry merengues again. They were so good."

Sydney's heart swelled at the compliment. "Thank you. I'd love to make them for you again. I guess I just want to work with nice people and make people happy. I know how to do that with food, sort of, and I don't know anything else."

"The sky's the limit, Sydney," Ward encouraged. "Whatever you want to do, it will be possible. Dream a little."

She nodded, overwhelmed by the idea. "As long as I

can see Ava on a regular basis, I'll be happy. I've missed you so much, Ava. Thank you for replying to the letter."

"Thanks for sending me a phone number. I've wanted to hear your voice so badly, Syd. I've considered breaking into the office to try to find contact information in my records, but I'm too much of a rule follower. I'd hate to get caught, and I really didn't want to accidentally talk to Belinda." She twisted her napkin. "Syd? Thanks for making sure I could stay at school. I know I just told you how miserable I've been, but I remember how awful Belinda was when I was little. I can't imagine what she's like now. Is Chantelle awful too? She has never written me, not that I expected her to."

Sydney shrugged and looked at Ward.

"What?" he asked, chuckling. "She's been a very mediocre but pleasant assistant since Belinda assigned her to me. You were right when you warned me she wasn't the smartest person, and she passed along a bit of misinformation that I let slip to her without thinking of the consequences, but she's fine."

Sydney laughed, and Ava watched them with wide eyes. "She works for you?" she asked Ward.

"For now," he replied.

Sydney said, "Chantelle is beautiful and entitled and only ever considers herself, but she's mostly harmless. She's not mean like her mom. Belinda burned all of the letters you've written me. I was hiding them under the floor in my room. She found them and burned them all in front of me."

"I'll write you more," Ava promised. "But I'll mail them to Ward, and he can keep them safe for you."

"I'd like that. You'll graduate soon?" Sydney asked as she finished her meal and leaned back in her chair, full for the first time in a long time.

"Yes. I'm ready to be done with school, but I'm also scared to leave. I've been here forever."

The waiter came and collected their plates and offered them dessert. Sydney didn't think she could fit anything else in her stomach, but she didn't want the evening to end, and the food had been so good. She ordered creme brûlée with enthusiasm.

Ward leaned forward again, his intense gaze focused on Ava. "You are both welcome, any time, to stay at my condo. I can always go crash with Ice. He lives in the same building a few floors down. It's not an imposition."

"Says you," Ice scoffed, laughing. "I'm kidding. Of course he's welcome at my place. Seriously."

Sydney blinked back the emotion squeezing her chest and making her eyes tear up. "Thank you."

"You, actually, might need to take me up on that, uh, today," Ward commented, clearing his throat. Sydney's curiosity was piqued, but she let it go. Knowing she had somewhere safe to go was enough for now. She focused on Ava.

"I'm sorry you haven't been getting acceptance letters. We'll figure it out. Gap years are popular, from what I hear."

The waiter returned once more with their desserts, and Sydney enjoyed hers just as much as she'd enjoyed the main course. She turned to Ward. "Thank you for this." She gestured to the table. "The food has been decadent. I'm not used to such fine things, and I appreciate it. Though I would've been just as happy at a McDonalds."

They all laughed. Ice admitted, "I don't think I've ever seen Ward eat at a McDonalds."

"It wasn't exactly a place I was allowed to go when I was a kid, and as an adult, I just can't bring myself to try it. The visions I have in my head of McDonalds are kids running around screaming and greasy food." He shrugged.

"Even with the downsides, I still would've been happy to eat there with all of you. This has been really nice," Sydney said.

Ava added, "We don't exactly have field trips to McDonalds here either. I'm not sure I've missed out on too much."

Ward changed the subject. "So, do you have a spring break coming up?"

Ava fiddled with her napkin. "Yes. It's a good time to catch up on homework. Almost everyone goes to Aspen or Miami or some other exotic place, and school is quiet." Sydney's heart hurt for Ava, being left out of adventures and being all alone. She wondered why Ward asked but didn't have to wait long for the answer.

"Assuming it's okay with Sydney, you're welcome to spend it together. I'm sure you could still get any homework done that you were hoping to finish."

Sydney shifted in her seat while Ava bounced in hers. Sydney was torn between excitement at time with

Ava and utter fear of what the Marshalls had in store. "What if ..." She couldn't quite formulate her thoughts, but the fear must have been clear on her face.

Ward put a hand over hers. "The Marshalls are losing their power over you. Trust me, Syd. I won't let you down."

She nodded. "I'm counting on that, and that's kind of scary too."

TWENTY-THREE

WARD

Too soon, Ava needed to get back to school. Ice took her, leaving Sydney with Ward. The night had gone better than he could have hoped for. He felt privileged to have been present at the girls' reunion. He couldn't imagine being separated from someone he cared about for over ten years, with only rare written communication.

Ward helped Sydney put her coat back on, and she turned and smiled at him, her eyes sparkling with joy.

"Please thank Marian for me. And thank you. It was nice to feel pretty tonight. Everything about tonight feels so extravagant and perfect."

Ward swallowed the lump in his throat at the reminder that he lived a privileged life. "It was nothing. Really. I'm glad you like what she chose for you. You're beautiful, no matter what you're wearing, but you've been glowing since you got here. Stunning." He watched a blush spread across her cheeks.

He thanked the waiter and the manager that came

out to see them off, and he led her out to the waiting car. Ward joined her in the back seat and sat close, wrapping her hand in his. She rested her head against his shoulder and closed her eyes.

"Thank you for finding my sister," she whispered. "Best day ever. I don't want it to end."

He rubbed his thumb across the back of her hand. "About that ... I don't want to take you back to the Marshalls'. Their world is crumbling around them, and I don't think it's safe for you to go back. Is there anything you need from there? Will you come home with me? I meant what I said earlier. I can crash with Ice if it would make you feel more comfortable."

Sydney was quiet for a long time. He wondered if she'd fallen asleep. Finally, she replied, "I could never kick you out of your own home, Ward."

"If you feel unsafe, you'll do just that. Promise me."

She lifted her head and glared at him with a fire that surprised him. "I've never felt unsafe with you before. Is there something I don't know?" she demanded.

Ward sighed and rested his head back on the head-rest. "No, of course not. But you've lived with things outside of your control for so long. I don't know what you need in order to feel safe."

She settled back against his shoulder and squeezed his hand. "I feel safe with you, Ward." After a moment, she added, "Belinda got rid of anything that reminded her of my dad. Or my mom, for that matter. I don't think there's anything left, especially now that my letters are gone too. There isn't anything irreplaceable."

Ward considered that. "Was that the house you lived in with your parents?" Sydney nodded. "Is it tainted now that Belinda and Tad have taken over, or is the house itself special to you?"

She shrugged, and then she sat up again and frowned at him. "What are you asking? No. You aren't going to do anything crazy."

He shrugged back. "Buying real estate isn't crazy. It's actually something I do all the time." He smirked at her, and she just shook her head.

"You're impossible," she muttered.

He couldn't help it. He wanted everything made right in her world. He wanted to see her smile, to know she felt free to do whatever she wanted, even if it meant she'd leave him behind. He just wanted her to be happy. "You never did answer the question," he prompted.

She didn't answer, but she swiped at her eyes. He nudged her up and took her face in his hands. He wiped away the tears leaking down her cheeks.

"I miss my dad," she whispered. "So much. I don't know if I'd feel him again if the house was free of them. I have to believe, though, that he's watching over me. That he nudged me into your path. I feel his hugs in yours."

Ward kissed her forehead and pulled her closer. He was buying the house. And if it didn't end up bringing her joy, he'd sell it or burn it to the ground. Whatever would give her closure.

The rest of the drive was quiet. Ward's mind whirled with what was to come over the next few days, and Sydney rested.

The driver stopped outside Ward's building and opened the door for them, helping Sydney out. Ward thanked him and walked her inside, across the lobby, and to the elevator. He pointed out Ice's floor before pressing the button for his own. He studied their reflection in the metal door of the elevator. They looked good together. She was stunning in her dress and wool coat, and he was grateful to Marian for finding something that suited her.

Ward unlocked his door and waved her inside, hoping he hadn't left a mess. He'd hoped she'd agree to come home with him, but he'd been busy before he left to go pick up Ava. She walked in tentatively at first, but she rushed to the windows overlooking the city. He tossed his keys on the counter and pulled off his tie, tossing his jacket over a chair. He walked up behind her and gently tugged on her coat, and she slipped her arms free. When she smiled back at him, his heart skipped a beat. "Make yourself at home," he said before forcing himself to step back. He hung up their coats in the entry closet.

When he got back, he found her curled up on his couch, her boots discarded on the floor. She had pulled the blanket from the back of the couch and looked cozy, flipping through a thriller novel he'd left on the side table.

She held it up and asked, "Is this yours or Ice's? It's in your house, but it seems like something he'd read."

Ward laughed out loud. "It is his, but I was reading it. We have similar tastes and trade back and forth."

"Hmm. Your own little book club." She giggled. He could just imagine what she was thinking: He and Ice sitting here with glasses of wine talking about books. It was ridiculous and it made him smile as much as her giggle had.

He flipped on the fireplace, filling the room with a warm glow. Sydney sighed in contentment. "Your place is lovely," she commented. "It could use a little color, or maybe a plant, but it's beautiful."

Ward shrugged and sat beside her. "It's home. It's functional." He relaxed in the quiet, watching the flicker of the fireplace. "I'll show you the rest in a little while. For now, this is nice."

Sydney nodded and moved a bit closer to lean on him. Neither felt the need to speak for a while, enjoying the peaceful evening. Ward wasn't surprised to hear the door open an hour later. Ice quietly walked in, took in the situation, and pulled Sydney up off the couch. Ward waited to see what he was up to.

"You're sure Ava's safe?" Sydney asked.

"Yes." He nodded. "Ward and I met with the headmaster, and I've met with their head of security. They're looking out for her. Ava has a phone with security on speed-dial. She's safe." It took him a moment of awkward silence to clear his throat. "You're safe too, Syd." He pulled the chain from around his neck, and Sydney gasped, her shoulders shuddering as Ice returned her ring to her, placing the chain gently back around her own neck.

She threw her arms around him and held tight. "Thank you. You kept it safe for me," she whispered.

"I keep my promises," he vowed as he pulled back. "The phone in your coat pocket also has her number saved, and ours. It also has the unit numbers and door codes for Ward's condo and mine, saved under contacts. You're welcome, any time, for any reason. If you need anything, ask."

She nodded, clutching her ring. "I can't imagine ever letting myself into your place, though, Ice. What if you have a date over?"

Ward expected him to laugh, to say, "okay, knock first" or something. But he didn't, and there was a vulnerability in Sydney's expression that sobered him. The seriousness on Ice's face had Ward standing but otherwise frozen, unsure what to do with himself.

"Syd," Ice took a breath, his voice quiet, "I know what it's like to grow up isolated. To be forced into being responsible too soon, with no one to rely on but yourself. So I'm going to tell you the things that it took me too long to accept. If you forget, I'll remind you. You aren't alone anymore. You aren't a burden. You are valuable. You are always welcome. The people who care about you will be there for you on good days and bad, for the little things and the big things. Don't ever hesitate to share how you're feeling or what you need. Even if what you need in the moment is to set up a prank in my condo that will make you laugh at my expense. Even if it interrupts a date. If I'm with someone who can't understand how important my friends are to me, I'd rather know that early in the relationship anyway."

Ward held out a hand to Sydney. She took it and held it tight. "Thanks, Ice. For everything."

Ice nodded and turned back to the door as if he

hadn't just stunned them both. "See you in the morning," he called on his way out.

After the door locked, it took Ward a full minute to recover. Ice didn't talk about himself much, about the things that mattered, and Ward wouldn't soon forget his words.

"How about I give you the rest of the tour?" He wrapped an arm around Sydney and led her to the open kitchen. She ran her hand along the granite countertop of the island in appreciation.

He showed her down the hall to the guest room, the bathroom, and then his room, where he left her in the doorway to grab something from his dresser for her to wear to sleep. He ducked into his bathroom to grab an extra toothbrush and toothpaste as well. Those little gift bags from the dentist every six months came in handy.

When he returned, she was leaning against the door-frame with her eyes closed. "Tired?" he asked with a chuckle.

"Mmm," she hummed as she nodded but didn't open her eyes. He put an arm around her again and gently nudged her to the bathroom.

He put everything on the counter and pulled her into a hug. Remembering what she'd said about feeling her dad when he hugged her felt like a heavy weight on his chest. He could only hope to be good enough. He pulled back and nudged her inside. "You know where to find me if you need me. Goodnight, Syd."

She blinked sleepily. "Goodnight, Ward."

TWENTY-FOUR
SYDNEY

Sydney went through the motions of getting ready for bed. As tired as she was, her mind wouldn't stop replaying the evening. Ava had grown up. She was beautiful and thoughtful and smart. And now Sydney could be there for her, talk to her, see her. They could tackle the future together. She took a deep breath, trying to settle the emotions rolling through her body. She'd hate for Ward to find her choking on her toothpaste.

Once ready for bed, Sydney turned off the bathroom light, walked into the guest room, and sat on the edge of the bed, her mind still on the events of the day. It had started just like any other, cooking breakfast, ignoring Chantelle's chatter and Belinda's barbs. Tad hadn't appeared, and she was sure that was for the best.

Thinking about them, though, and sitting in a dark room, a chill swept over Sydney. The darkness was too much, and she sat frozen, panic swelling up within her. She was freezing, shaking, and she didn't realize she was sobbing until Ward sat beside her and tentatively wrapped an arm around her. His warmth snapped her back to reality, and she felt foolish. She wasn't in the dark, cold basement. She wasn't alone and trapped. She swiped the tears from her cheeks and whispered, "I'm sorry. I'm okay."

Ward didn't comment for a long time. He just held her until she pulled herself together. He didn't ask, but she knew he deserved an explanation. She ran through the words in her head, several times, weighing if she could say them. If she should say them. All the while, Ward remained steady, his thumb gently moving in a slow, steady rhythm on her shoulder.

She slowed her breathing and blurted, "I was locked in the basement. That week I was gone. In the dark. With nothing. I found an emergency kit, but they locked me down there not caring if I died of dehydration. They're awful, Ward."

He stilled as she spoke, and when she'd finished, he abruptly stormed out of the room, leaving her confused and lost. He'd at least turned on the light in the hallway on his way out. She heard the racket of things being carelessly moved around but didn't follow him to investigate. He came back minutes later with a desk lamp, which he plugged in, set on the nightstand, and turned on to the lowest setting. A soft glow warmed the room, vanquishing the darkness. Ward knelt in front of her. "They'll pay, Sydney," he vowed. "I'm so glad you're okay. You're the strongest, most resourceful person I know."

She didn't feel strong. "I'm afraid of the dark," she whispered.

"That's understandable. Thank you for telling me. Is there anything else I can do to help you sleep?"

She shook her head. She was well past the point of exhaustion. "Thank you. Goodnight again," she offered with a small smile.

He squeezed her hand and stood. "Night, Syd."

She climbed under the covers as he left the room, and she was asleep soon after her head hit the pillow.

Sydney woke in the most comfortable bed she'd ever slept in. The mattress was huge and firm but comfortable. The sheets were luxuriously soft, and the duvet was warm and cozy. Of the several pillows on the bed, she found one that was just the right level of soft. She'd slept better than ever and didn't want to start the day. Sunlight streamed in through the curtains, and she glanced at her watch.

She sat up with a jolt when she realized it was eleven. She didn't think she'd ever slept that long. Perhaps when she'd been a small child. She got up and stretched and made her way to the bathroom. She could hear Ward's voice down the hall. On the bathroom counter, she found a sweatshirt that looked like Ward's and a t-shirt and leggings that still had tags on, along with a pair of new women's socks. She pondered that while she got ready for the day and changed. It was disconcerting to not have the routine of breakfast to cook or work to rush off to.

She joined Ward in the kitchen just as he ended a call. He looked comfortable in jeans and a sweatshirt, sitting at the kitchen island with his laptop open. He smiled when he saw her. "There is a bag with more clothes by the couch. Marian did a little online shopping and had it delivered this morning."

Sydney smiled and blushed. "That was nice of her."

Ward chuckled. "Yes, it was. When she left on medical leave to care for her sister, she made me swear I wouldn't call her, but now that I've asked her for help buying clothing for you, I keep getting messages." He unlocked his phone and scrolled to his message thread with Marian and turned it to show Sydney. This morning, she'd sent several asking if Sydney liked her choices, if they'd fit, and if she needed anything else.

Sydney took his phone and replied.

> This is Sydney. Thank you so much for choosing such lovely clothes. They fit great. I hope to be able to meet you sometime.

Marian immediately sent a text back with a gif of an excited puppy jumping up and down, making Sydney laugh and Ward shake his head. "I think my assistant is broken. She has never done or said anything remotely joyful before."

Sydney eyed him. "Were you maybe not so nice to her?" she ventured a guess, based on Chantelle's musings about him being awfully cold for someone so hot.

He turned on his stool and took his phone back, placing his hands on her waist. "I might have a reputation for being ... mean to my assistants. I plan to be better when Marian comes back."

"But you'll keep up the mean streak for Chantelle?" she asked, curious.

He studied her for a minute. "I've considered firing her every day, especially after she leaked information, but I don't have the energy to deal with a new assistant, and I'm supposed to be setting a better example. It will be even harder knowing that she did nothing to help you." He sighed. "I'm hiding all of my actual work from her so she can't mess anything up. Especially as my most pressing new project involves her family."

Sydney sat on the stool beside him and sighed. "I've been avoiding asking you about that, but I should probably face it. What is going on?" she asked, tension building in her shoulders.

Ward stood. "First, breakfast." Sydney started to rise, but Ward stopped her, his eyebrows raised. "Do you drink coffee? Tea? Hot chocolate?" He pulled a mug down from the cabinet and brought her a small basket full of K-cups for his single serving coffee maker. Sydney pulled it closer and looked through the assortment while he filled the water reservoir. She found one that sounded good and held it out to him, but she stood and watched him start her coffee so she'd know how to make her own later.

He opened the fridge and started moving things around. "Creamer?" he asked, pulling out a small carton of French vanilla creamer. It sounded decadent. She was used to grabbing burned black coffee from the diner.

"Sure," she replied, taking it from him while he continued to rummage. He listed off the contents of his fridge to figure out what to make for breakfast. She laughed and said, "You don't have to wait on me, Ward. You said I should make myself at home."

He cupped her face with his hands, and a dark look crossed his face. "I have the feeling no one did nice things for you. I don't want you to feel like you have to cook and serve and clean here," he grumbled earnestly.

She wrapped her arms around him. His thoughtfulness touched her, and it took a moment for her to get a grip and respond. "Thank you," she said, looking up into his stormy eyes. "Unless you plan to be demanding and ignore me instead of saying thank you once in a while, I'd like to cook for you and clean up after myself. It's the least I can do."

"You don't owe me anything, Syd. Not a single thing."

"We can agree to disagree." Determined, she moved him aside and inspected his fridge. "I am starving, though. It's lunchtime already." There wasn't much in his fridge. Milk, eggs, bread, cheese, and what looked like a case of protein drinks. Sydney laughed. "I think some shopping will be in order. Want eggs, even though it's lunchtime?" she asked with a smile.

Ward's lips turned up in a smile, and he said, "Sure. I guess Ice and I eat out a lot." He pulled out his phone and focused on it while Sydney found her way around his kitchen and made some simple scrambled eggs with cheese. She grilled the bread with lots of butter and made egg sandwiches like they did at the diner. There was no way something so unhealthy would've been tolerated at home, and she enjoyed every bite sitting beside Ward. The coffee was rich and a little sweet, and even though Ward was focused on his laptop while he ate, she was content. Happy.

After she washed up the dishes, she made herself a second cup of coffee and rejoined him. She hadn't forgotten that he hadn't answered her question earlier. She nudged his shoulder. He looked over and grinned. "Not going to let it go, are you?"

Sydney shook her head. "I want to. I want to just sit here with you with no responsibilities and nowhere to be, thinking about my sister and how good it was to see her. But it's my life you're poking around in, and I should know what's going on."

Ward reached out and moved a lock of hair behind her ear. "I have a little story for you, then. Someone I went to college with approached me a while back with a business proposition. He wanted me to finance a building project. The project was interesting. I liked the location and the planned use of the new structure he was proposing. But his company wasn't doing well. He needed the money because his other projects were bleeding cash, and he hadn't invested wisely."

"You didn't agree to give him money," she guessed, following along.

"No. Instead I decided to maintain my ruthless reputation. I picked up another piece of property practically next door and developed a strikingly similar project on a fast-tracked timeline."

Sydney's eyes widened. "Wow, okay. Don't make you mad, got it," she replied with a laugh.

Tension released from Ward's shoulders, and he smiled. "I took it another step further and started investigating all the investments in his portfolio and his projects in development. I found something interesting. He had been investing heavily into each of Tad's businesses."

Sydney frowned in confusion. "Really? I didn't even know he had investors. He always bragged about how well each business was doing."

"Smoke and mirrors," he replied. "Some are doing better than others. Honestly, they're not great investments. But I've been methodically buying out the other parties for most of the investor's projects and investments. I pulled the trigger on all of them a few days ago, leaving him with nothing but his investments in the restaurants. I pushed him out of everything else, and he relinquished those last investments for pennies on the dollar. Two days ago, Tad found out he now owes me all of the money he borrowed from Tate, and I exercised the option in the contracts to call them all due immediately. He can't pay, of course, and now the restaurants and the event center are mine. Well, they belong to McKinney Enterprises."

Sydney sat with that for a minute. When the full implication hit, she smiled. "Tad doesn't own them anymore. He has nothing?"

"As far as I can tell, they were everything he owned. A little brutal, perhaps, but I felt it was necessary."

"And you closed them all down? How is that good for your investment?"

Ward shook his head. "Just for a few days. I have meetings lined up with the managers to go over changes to make, profitability, reopening plans. I'd like your input, Syd. You know these places, and I'm sure you have ideas for how we can improve them. We'll try to make them better, and then we'll decide whether to keep them or sell them off."

Ward's phone buzzed on the counter. When he answered, he stepped out of the kitchen. Sydney could hear yelling through the phone, even from across the room. Ward didn't say much as he listened and paced the living room, his shoulders tight and knuckles white on the phone.

When he returned, he wrapped Sydney in a hug, the tension draining from his body. "It was worth it, no matter what," he whispered.

The rest of the day, Ward walked Sydney through what he knew of each of the establishments. He listened intently, taking notes, when she shared what she saw as problems and opportunities at each one. Talking about Keller was easy. She enjoyed the variety of events and the different challenges each brought. She would never again have to staff an impossible event by herself. She had so many ideas for how the extra rooms could be used, and brainstorming with Ward was fun.

The diner was easy to talk about too. Black was not,

but Ward's steadiness encouraged her to tell him everything she could.

Ward shared that the manager of Walnut Alley had already been vocal about changes they wanted. They had constantly clashed with Tad about what direction to go. They were relieved to see Tad removed from the picture and to gain some freedom back.

Sydney could relate. Hope bloomed in her chest. Hope that this was real, that she'd never have to see Tad again. That it could be normal to get a full night's sleep in a warm bed. That she could rely on someone other than herself. The longer they talked, the more it sank in that she was free. She would have actual paychecks deposited to her own bank account. She could go anywhere she wanted, buy what she wanted, spend time how she wanted to. She couldn't stop smiling.

At the end of the day, Sydney padded into the living room with a cup of tea, ready to curl up in her new favorite spot on the couch at Ward's side. He'd been relaxed most of the day, but now tension radiated from him once more, stopping her in her tracks. He reached out a hand to her, and she sat, pulling her legs up underneath her and placing her tea on the table.

"What's wrong?" she asked.

He shook his head and held her hand. "I'm angry that you had to deal with them for so many years. How did you do it?"

She settled in closer to him and sipped her tea. She could handle his anger and frustration over her past. It was over now, and she didn't have to worry about them anymore. "I reminded myself that Ava needed me to keep going. And it wasn't always this bad. I've worked hard, and I didn't have luxuries, or, I guess, heat." She paused at Ward's growl. "But these last few months have been the worst. Maybe it's because she was going to graduate and they realized they wouldn't have anything to threaten me with, or maybe it was just business stress from the loans you were talking about."

"That's no excuse for the things they've done."

"No, it isn't. But I'm okay now. And Ava is safe. That's all that matters to me."

Ward adjusted too easily to having Sydney in his space. He enjoyed having her nearby, and he valued her input. She may have been stuck as a dishwasher most of the time, but she saw and heard things. She had a good mind for what improvements could be made, especially at Keller.

On the third day of the restaurant closure, Ward, Sydney, and Ice arrived at Keller bright and early. They set up rows upon rows of chairs in the main event space, but there would be standing room only if everyone showed up.

Ward watched everyone filter in, some clustering in small groups talking. Others took a seat quietly and observed the room. Many seemed nervous, and Ward felt a bit of guilt that these people had probably been worrying for three days that they were about to be fired.

Ward walked up to the microphone. "Take a seat, please, everyone," he said. He spotted Sydney in the front row on the end. He hadn't shared exactly what he had planned, but she knew she could continue to work wherever she wanted. "Take a seat," Ward repeated. More employees made their way to chairs and sat down. Some stood back along the walls.

Ward waited a beat before trying to start the meeting. He looked over the faces of the restless employees. "For those who don't know me, my name is Ward McKinney. I represent the new ownership group of the restaurants previously owned by Tad Marshall, including Keller. I intend to reopen them all, and you'll all be paid for the three days of closure. I apologize for the abruptness and lack of transparency, and for the mess I know kitchen staff will need to sort through to clear out and restock expired foods. I know that these businesses can do well, and when they do well, the employees will too. That said, there will be changes. If you work at the diner, please stand." A couple dozen people stood, including Sydney.

"Those of you standing, if you also work at any of the other restaurants or here at Keller, please sit." A few, including Sydney, sat back down. "The rest of you standing, please pick up a packet along the back wall. The diner has been doing well just as it is. There won't be any big changes. The packets detail the reopening schedule and some benefit changes. Feel free to reach out to your manager if you have questions. You're excused."

There was some chatter as the diner employees made their way out. "Is there anyone who works exclusively here at Keller?" he asked. No one rose. "Okay. There won't be big changes here either, but it does sit empty more than it should, so we'll be working on that. Would those who work at Walnut Alley stand, please?"

About half of the remaining employees stood. "If you also work at Black, please sit back down." A few sat. "The rest of you, your manager is waiting in the room next door. There are some changes planned to improve the restaurant. If you also work at the diner, please pick up a packet from the back on your way over there. Thank you." He waited while they all filed out, a few stopping to get diner packets.

"What about the people that aren't here today?" someone shouted.

Ward nodded. "Good question. Managers will be following up with anyone they don't see. There will be a limited time for them to respond before it will be assumed that they have quit. So the rest of you work at Black, correct?" He saw a number of them nod and heard a few yeses.

"Black has some problems." He heard some chuckles and some scoffs in the audience. "The illegal stuff will stop." The room went silent. "If anyone was thriving in the illegal side of the business, I suggest you disappear before this meeting is over. I will not stand for that in any of these establishments. I'm going to turn the meeting over to Black's managers who will fill you in on the rest of the changes. Let them know if you have questions or concerns. Thank you for being here today."

He stepped away and realized Sydney had slipped to the back of the room at some point. She held a diner packet in her hand. "I don't want to go back to Black," she whispered. He nodded and took her hand. The managers would handle everything from here, and Ice had security on hand to lock up once everyone left.

They walked out into the cool, mid-morning air with Ice right behind them. Ward led Sydney into a coffee shop and grabbed a quiet table. Once they all had warm cups of caffeine, Sydney said, "It seems like it went well."

Ward nodded.

Ice added, "Ready for part two of the day?"

"Part two?" Sydney asked.

Ward smiled. "The next thing on my calendar today is to fire Belinda and Chantelle. I'd like you to be there. This will sound crazy, but the idea brings me great joy. Hear me out." His heart pounded in his chest. He'd done dozens of multi-million dollar deals without the nerves that now made his hand tremble. He took a deep breath before continuing. "Consider agreeing to be my fiancé."

Sydney stiffened, and her eyes widened. "What?"

"Ward," Ice warned.

The more Ward thought about it, the more he wanted it. He took her hands in his. "I'm not saying I think we should get married after living together for a few days."

"I would hope not," Ice grumbled.

Ward ignored him, focused on Sydney. "But the next priority is petitioning the court for guardianship of Ava. I've spoken with a family law attorney. If we were engaged, you'd have my financial stability. It would be clear to the judge that you could support Ava, making it an easy decision for them to give you guardianship. I also don't want there to be any doubt in Tad or Belinda's minds that you are not alone or vulnerable. They have no power over you or Ava anymore."

Sydney's gaze flicked to Ice. "Is he serious?" Ward tensed and squeezed her hand. "I don't see how this is good for you, Ward. You getting engaged would be huge news, and later changing your mind would be a scandal."

"I'm not changing my mind. I love you, Sydney. The moment I met you changed my life. I know it's fast, and I'm not saying any of this to make you feel trapped or pressured. That's the last thing I would ever want you to feel. I want you to have the freedom and space to choose what you want your future to look like. If I'm ultimately not in it, I just want you to be happy."

"If I say no?" she whispered.

The thought caused physical pain in his chest, and he swallowed hard. "Nothing changes in the short term," he promised, the catch in his voice betraying his confidence. "I plan to do everything in my power to make sure Ava is safe and that both of you have what you need to move forward."

"And if I say yes?"

"I'd get the honor of being by your side." After a moment, he whispered, "Please say yes, Syd." He held his breath and watched emotions flit across her face.

She studied him for a long moment before nodding and saying, "Yes."

Ward's heart jumped, and a joyful smile spread across his face. "You won't regret this." He brought his hand up to cup her cheek and leaned forward, close enough to feel her breath mingling with his.

Ice cleared his throat and broke the spell of the moment. "I hope you're planning to propose to her again properly, somewhere better than a coffee shop."

Sydney giggled. "That won't be necessary."

Ward looked around and shrugged. "Maybe, but it won't involve a thousand roses. I have no regrets." Ward didn't let go of her hand as they finished their coffees.

As they exited the shop, he turned left, and Ice muttered, "The office is that way."

Ward just nodded and opened the door of a jewelry store a few doors down. "We have a purchase to make first."

Sydney hesitated in the doorway. "You're serious," she stated, as if she hadn't quite believed it.

"Absolutely. Let's find something that suits you."

The salesperson was thrilled to pull out some of her favorite pieces. She showed them some of the flashiest diamonds she had, but Sydney's eye gravitated to something more understated. Less ostentatious. As much as he wanted a beacon on her finger, she needed something she'd feel comfortable wearing. They settled on something sparkly but not huge, something Ward was proud to buy for her, yet something she wouldn't be afraid to wear. Ward was vaguely aware of Ice taking a picture of them as Ward slipped the ring on Sydney's shaking finger.

He held on to her hand and took a moment to absorb the enormity of what they were doing. Everything about this felt right, deep in his soul.

"Ward?" Sydney whispered, drawing his attention. "Second thoughts?"

He shook his head. "Not for a moment. You?"

"No." They stared at each other, drawing closer until their lips were a breath apart. He held back, giving her the opportunity to pull away. When she leaned closer, he couldn't stop himself from brushing his lips against hers.

The contact drew a whimper from Sydney and sent a shockwave through Ward. The kiss deepened, and Ward was gone. Home. He pulled back and smiled. The blush on Sydney's cheeks and her dazed expression told him he wasn't the only one affected. The love he felt for her wrapped around his heart and squeezed hard.

Ice quietly asked, "Ready to go?" They both waited for Sydney's nod. "Congrats, you two," he added, clapping Ward's shoulder before ushering them out onto the sidewalk toward the office.

Ward couldn't stop smiling, even as he walked through the McKinney building lobby. He took the opportunity to kiss Sydney again in the elevator, and Ice good-naturedly muttered, "Get a room."

They stepped off the elevator, and Ward kept Sydney's hand in his. They walked across the office, and Ward enjoyed the look of shock and confusion on Chantelle's face as she realized who walked by his side. "Join us in my office, Chantelle," he commanded. She nodded and stumbled as she tried to stand and follow them. She regained her footing quickly enough and joined them as Ice was calling down to HR to have Belinda sent up.

"Have a seat," he said, gesturing Chantelle to sit in one of the chairs across from his desk. She sat, still watching Sydney carefully. Ward sat in his chair and kept a hold of Sydney's hand. She stood beside him, watching Chantelle.

"I don't understand. How do you know each other?" Chantelle asked, a bit of a tremor in her voice.

He just waited, and soon enough, Belinda took a step in and halted in her tracks. Her gaze took in Sydney's appearance from head to toe. When Ward cleared his throat, she hesitantly sat beside Chantelle.

Ward didn't waste any time. "You're both here because you've acted against the best interests of this company. Chantelle, you shared information that was confidential to this office, and you, Belinda, attempted to exploit that information. Neither of you are employed here any longer." He paused for a beat. "I'm not without a heart, though. There are openings at Black, if you find yourselves in need of work."

Both of them gaped at him. Belinda was the first to recover her wits. "You must be joking! You can't fire me. I'm in HR. I know the rules. And what is she doing here?" she demanded.

Ward tilted his head. "My fiancé?" Sydney put her hand on Ward's shoulder, allowing the ring to sparkle in the light. He didn't need to add anything else.

Belinda choked and jumped out of her seat. She whirled around and stormed out of the office. Chantelle sat frozen at first. "You were supposed to want *me*," she whimpered, distraught. She stood slowly, and she stared at the ring and back at Ward. "I don't understand." When he had nothing more to add, she left, trailed by Ice.

Ward pulled Sydney onto his lap. "I found that satisfying. You?"

Sydney nodded and relaxed for a moment before pushing back and standing. "I'm sure you have work to do. I'll see you at home?"

Home. He liked the sound of that.

TWENTY-SIX
SYDNEY

Sydney took a few steps toward the door and turned back. Ward was watching her, a relaxed smile on his face. Her heart raced, and she smiled back, feeling heat in her cheeks. This was real. The weight on her finger was real.

She reminded herself that Ward had work to do and stepped out of his office, only to be embraced by an older woman wearing jeans, a tailored linen jacket, and modest heels.

"You must be Sydney," she gushed, pulling back. "I'm so glad to meet you!"

Ward called, "Marian, you're back?" Surprise colored his voice.

So this was the assistant Chantelle was filling in for. Her timing couldn't have been better.

"I've been home for a few days, and I was planning to come back to work next week, but Oliver strongly suggested I pop in this afternoon. I'm so glad I did."

Sydney smirked at Ice's discomfort over the use of his given name. He didn't say anything, but he didn't have to. His scowl spoke for itself.

Chantelle sniffled as she placed her things in a box, deliberately, one at a time.

Sydney focused on Marian. "Thank you so much for the lovely clothes you chose for me. I love them."

"Any time, dear. I would love to go shopping with you sometime, if you would like to. My daughter moved to Paris a few years ago, and I don't have anyone to shop with anymore. Maybe Mrs. McKinney would even join us."

"I would love that," Sydney replied. She blinked away the emotion building behind her eyes. She could imagine an idyllic afternoon of shopping and lunch. She missed having a mom, and she wouldn't turn down the opportunity to spend time with Marian and Ward's stepmom.

Ward squeezed Sydney's shoulder. "I'll get back to work, but I'm glad to see you, Marian, and I'm happy to have you back whenever you're ready." He turned back into his office.

"I need to be going too. I'll get your number from Ward and text you later, if that's okay?" Sydney asked Marian.

"Any time, Sydney," Marian replied with a cheerful wave.

Chantelle picked up her box and shuffled toward the elevator. Sydney took a deep breath and considered if she should take the elevator with her or wait. She didn't know what to say, but Chantelle didn't seem upset with her, just sad. Ice got into the elevator with them and pressed the lobby button.

"I've never seen Marian in *jeans*," Ice grumbled as the elevator doors closed.

Chantelle sniffed, her nose red. "Sydney?" She glanced at Ice but turned her gaze to the floor, her voice quiet. "I don't know what to do now. I didn't know I did something wrong. Mom said it was fine because we both worked at the same company. And Tad was arrested last night. I don't understand what's happening."

Sydney's heart twisted. It wasn't Chantelle's fault that Tad and Belinda were terrible people. It wasn't even her fault that she believed Belinda when she promised that Ward would love her. Belinda raised her to be obedient and trusting, not to think for herself. "Tad was doing illegal things, so I'm glad he was arrested. I feel safer knowing that. Thank you for telling me. You'll find another job, Chantelle. You can work with me at Keller, if you want." She wasn't sure where the offer came from, but she wouldn't take it back.

Chantelle nodded, and a tear slipped down her cheek. "I'm sorry Mom was so awful to you, Sydney. I'm sorry I didn't know how to help you."

"I survived. I'll be okay. It wasn't your fault."

The elevator doors opened in the lobby, and Ice followed them out, watching Chantelle carefully. Sydney stopped her and exchanged phone numbers. She wasn't sure they'd ever be real friends, but Sydney felt strangely protective of Chantelle. Maybe it was her forlorn expression, the absence of her usual sparkle. Losing her job, knowing her mom just lost her job as well, and seeing Tad get arrested were shaking up her whole world.

"Sydney, wait a minute." Ice stopped her from leaving the building with Chantelle. He pulled out his phone and started texting. When he put it back in his pocket, he looked up. "Paparazzi are gathering out front. Belinda must have tipped them off. They're not usually out there in the middle of the afternoon. There will be a car for you out front in a minute." He watched the front doors, standing in front of her.

Sydney peered around him and could see a few men with cameras standing around outside. Every time someone passed through the doors, they reached for their cameras.

"Ignore them," Ice advised. "I'll walk you straight to the car. If you say anything at all, say 'no comment.' You don't have to say anything. You and Ward can publish an official announcement on your own terms. Ready?"

Sydney nodded. She was as ready as she would ever be. She wrapped her arms around herself, tucking her left hand under her right arm, hiding her ring. Ice bustled her out to the car and past the photographers so quickly that they barely threw their questions at her before she was safely sealed in the car and whisked away to Ward's condo. Home.

A FEW WEEKS LATER, Sydney pulled a fresh batch of muffins from the oven just as the front door opened and Ava burst into the condo with Ward on her heels, a small smile on his face.

"Sydney!" Ava exclaimed, grabbing her sister in a hug the second the hot pan was safely on the stovetop. "I missed you!"

Sydney bear-hugged her back. "I missed you too!" She smacked Ward's hand away from the muffins without missing a beat. "They're hot." She laughed.

Ava whirled around and gave herself a tour of the place, flitting from room to room, leaving Sydney a moment to tip her head back for a quick kiss. "Did she have this much energy the whole way home?"

"She was actually pretty quiet until we walked through the door."

In moments, Ava was back and poked her head in the fridge. "Nice place, Ward," she said, pulling out a carton of juice.

"Thanks. Make yourself at home." She already seemed perfectly comfortable. It warmed Sydney's heart. It had been so long since Ava had an actual home to return to.

The guilt would eat away at Sydney if she let it. Ava's only semblance of family for the past ten years had been classmates and teachers. People who not only didn't care to get to know her but actively made her life difficult. Seeing her free and happy here, in this place where Sydney felt safe and loved, meant everything to her. It was all Ward. He exuded confidence and warmth.

"What would you like to do this week?" she asked Ava, who had just shoved half of a hot muffin in her mouth and was waving her hand in front of her face frantically.

A drink of juice later, Ava said, "I have a whole list!" She rushed out of the room and was back moments later with a notebook and a pen. She wasn't kidding. She had a list of every attraction in Seattle.

Sydney and Ward's eyes both widened. "Um," Ward started, "I don't think it's possible to see all of these things in a week."

"Of course not," she replied with an eyeroll. "They're in order. We can see the rest over the summer!" She looked between them, and vulnerability crept into her expression. "Can't we?" Her small voice was such a stark contrast to her energy moments earlier.

"Anything you want," Ward reassured her when Sydney couldn't speak over the lump in her throat.

She pulled Ava's list closer. "Good ideas, Ava. I've wanted to do these things too." The zoo, the aquarium, Pike Place market, and riding a ferry topped the list. "It's supposed to be nice for the next few days, so it should be a great time for outdoor things."

"Today, though," Ava said, "can we just chill?" She yawned and stretched. "I'm happy to be here." *Away from school* was implied.

Sydney pulled her back into a hug and just held on to her. Ava rested her head on her sister's shoulder and breathed deeply. Sydney leaned back against the counter, taking Ava's relaxed weight. She ran her hand up and down Ava's back as she had when she'd been a little girl. After a while, Sydney whispered, "There's mint chocolate ice cream in the freezer."

Ava jolted upright and pulled the pint from the freezer. Sydney handed her a spoon and a napkin. "Can we watch movies? I have a list." She flipped to another page in her notebook filled with movie titles.

Sydney readily agreed. Another day to rest before tackling Ava's tourism list sounded perfect.

"How have the last few weeks of school gone?" Ward asked over pizza a few movies and snack breaks later.

Ava bounced in her seat. "I'm sure you can imagine. My classmates are so predictable. When word got out that *my* sister is engaged to *the* Ward McKinney, the boys suddenly wanted to ask me out. I know they just want to meet you. I brush them off. The girls still just whisper about me—loudly. They're jealous, I guess, and unhappy you're off the market, but seriously? No offense Ward, but you're old."

Sydney choked on a laugh. "He's only a few years older than me."

Ava stared back at her, dead serious. "I hate to break it to you, but you're old too, sis."

Old? At twenty-six? Her sister might kick off a quarter-life crisis. Her mouth opened and closed, and no words came out.

"You aren't old," Ward whispered near her ear. His phone buzzed, and he pulled away to glance at it. He cleared his throat. "I have news that you'll both want to hear." At his seriousness, both girls sobered. "I've been looking into the house."

"Ward," Sydney sighed. "I'm pretty sure I told you the house isn't important."

Ava looked back and forth between them, confusion knitting her brows. Sydney elaborated, "Dad's house, that Tad and Belinda took over. Ward wanted to buy it. It isn't necessary."

"You're right," he agreed, and Sydney's gaze snapped back to his. "You're right, because the house didn't pass to Belinda when your dad died. It belongs to the two of you."

"What?" She couldn't have heard right. "How is that possible?"

He shrugged. "Public record says the house is owned by a trust. It's taken a while to track down information on that, but your dad must have set it up before he died. You two are the beneficiaries. I found the attorney, and you'll be able to meet with her this week to find out the details."

Shock didn't quite describe Sydney's reaction. She couldn't comprehend that the house was hers. Tad and Belinda had acted like they'd owned it all this time. They'd treated Sydney like a nuisance, a slave, when she was actually the one that owned it? The more she thought about it, the angrier she got. She could have been living there on her own, working on her own terms, with Ava at home. She'd lost all of those years, for what?

Ward grabbed her in a bear hug and whispered, "You okay?"

She shook her head. No, she wasn't okay. She was angrier than she had ever been. She didn't want the house. She had a home here. But the feeling of being taken advantage of, robbed of time with her sister, robbed of peace, overwhelmed her.

"I'd fantasized about burning it to the ground. We can still do that, if you want," he shared, quiet enough that Ava wouldn't hear. It startled a laugh from Sydney and pulled her out of her downward spiral.

<hr>

"SYDNEY?" Ava asked after they'd talked about everything and nothing for over an hour, facing each other in Sydney's bed. "Why are you in here with me when your adoring fiancé is in the next room? Is it because you think I can't handle hearing you two together? Because my roommate has been sneaking her boyfriend in at night all year and they are *not* quiet."

Sydney's mind spun through all of that information. "Eww! Your roommate and her boyfriend ... really?"

"Don't dodge the question."

"I'm not, I'm just ... horrified for you. All year? We should have them move you."

"No! Don't. It'll be worse if we make a big deal about it. Don't worry. Ice is my hero. He got me a phone and earbuds, and I don't hear them anymore. It's fine. So?" She poked her sister's arm every few seconds while she waited for an answer.

Sydney traced the stitches in the quilt and debated with herself about how to answer.

"You are engaged for real, right?" Ava asked in a small voice. "This isn't just a 'save Ava' ploy that will fall apart—"

"It's real," Sydney rushed to reassure her. "It's real. It's just been fast, that's all."

"Are you having second thoughts?" Ava traced the ring on Sydney's finger.

Was she? She didn't have any doubts about Ward. She was happy here with him. She felt loved, and she loved him in return. She lit up at the mere sound of his voice. Her doubts were within herself. "What can I possibly offer him?" she whispered, letting her insecurity loose.

Ava shoved her shoulder. "Seriously? You're the best sister in the world. He's so lucky to have you. You love big and show it. You take care of everyone you love. What more could he possibly need?"

THEY MADE the most of spring break doing some of the things they'd missed out on over the years. They watched movies late into the night, eating popcorn and ice cream and laughing. They went to the zoo and the aquarium and visited bookstores and craft stores. They tried on clothes and enjoyed silly choices just as much as figuring out what they truly liked. They chose homey decorations to warm up Ward's condo, and he humored them.

The paparazzi followed them around for a while. They published photos of Sydney and Ava and a few more of the happy couple after their engagement was announced. Their interest died down when they realized Ward was serious and wouldn't be giving them fresh photo ops with new dates every night anymore.

To the surprise of no one, the news reported that Tad was critically injured while in jail. Whoever he was selling drugs for clearly didn't want him talking.

It was painful to take Ava back to school, but graduation would come up quickly, and she'd be home again. Ward hadn't uttered a word of complaint in the week that Ava spent with them.

Sydney enjoyed being alone with him again, getting to know him better. She loved his willingness to go do whatever came to mind, even if she wanted to go shopping. She wasn't a shopper, but she did find that she enjoyed trying things on and seeing his reaction. She loved the way he always had his arm around her or held her hand when they were out and about or even at home. She loved the way he accepted Ava and insisted he was as anxious as Sydney was for her graduation. She couldn't imagine her life without him. It wasn't the condo or the money. He was her home, her steadying anchor, and her sail.

Home meant something special to Sydney again. Home was a place where she felt loved and free to be herself. Home was a place to spend time with people who would drop everything to help if something was wrong, and who could just hang out without the pressure of a spotless house.

Her dad had always told her that fairytales weren't real. That a prince wouldn't sweep her off her feet. That relationships took work, but that they were worth it when you found the right person. Sydney thought her dad would approve of Ward, and she was determined to live her happily ever after.

AFTERWORD

Thank you for reading Ward and Sydney's story! I hope you've enjoyed it. Honest reviews are always appreciated.

I think Ice deserves his own happily-ever-after, don't you? I'm excited to share his story with you next in Intercepting Katie.

If you'd like to receive updates and special content (including special scenes and letters from Ava), please click jesihaynes.com to sign up for my newsletter.

Thanks again! Your support means everything.

McKinney Enterprises of Seattle

Intercepting Sydney

Intercepting Katie

Flannigans of Seattle (coming soon)

Intercepting Maura

Intercepting Bree

Intercepting Sara

New Hope Seattle (coming soon)

Intercepting Casey

Intercepting Tara